'The only other option,' Eliot said tonelessly, 'is for me to be in the same position as Ryan's mum. Married. So I can offer Ryan the same kind of stable home, with two parents.'

Why did the idea of Eliot marrying someone else make her feel as if someone were dissecting her heart with a rusty knife?

'…completely mad.'

'What?' She'd missed most of what he'd just said.

'I said, at three o'clock this morning I thought of the perfect solution, but it was completely mad. You'll say no, so there's no point in asking.'

'No to what?' she asked, mystified.

'Marrying me.'

No down-on-one-knee, no declaration of love, no nothing. He didn't even look as if he was saying something out of the ordinary. No, he probably hadn't even said that. It had been a mixture of wishful thinking and—

She blinked, hoping to clear her head. 'Did you just ask me to marry you?'

Kate Hardy lives on the outskirts of Norwich with her husband, two small children, two lazy spaniels—and too many books to count! She wrote her first book at six, when her parents gave her a typewriter for her birthday. She had the first of a series of sexy romances published at twenty-five, and swapped a job in marketing communications for freelance health journalism when her son was born, so she could spend more time with him. She's wanted to write for Mills & Boon® since she was twelve—and when she was pregnant with her daughter her husband pointed out that writing Medical Romances™ would be the perfect way to combine her interest in health issues with her love of good stories. It really is the best of both worlds—especially as she gets to meet a gorgeous new hero every time…

Recent titles by the same author:

A BABY OF HER OWN
HIS EMERGENCY FIANCÉE
HER SPECIAL CHILD
THE ITALIAN DOCTOR'S PROPOSAL
THE DOCTOR'S RESCUE
THE HEART CONSULTANT'S LOVER

THE REGISTRAR'S CONVENIENT WIFE

BY
KATE HARDY

For Phil G, with much love

All the characters in this book have no existence outside the imagination of the author, and have no relation whatsoever to anyone bearing the same name or names. They are not even distantly inspired by any individual known or unknown to the author, and all the incidents are pure invention.

MILLS & BOON and
MILLS & BOON with the Rose Device
are registered trademarks of the publisher.

First published in Great Britain 2004
Large Print edition 2005
Harlequin Mills & Boon Limited,
Eton House, 18-24 Paradise Road,
Richmond, Surrey TW9 1SR

© Pamela Brooks 2004

ISBN 0 263 18457 9

Set in Times Roman 16½ on 17½ pt.
17-0405-51324

Printed and bound in Great Britain
by Antony Rowe Ltd, Chippenham, Wiltshire

CHAPTER ONE

'IF I wasn't just back from honeymoon, I'd be tempted,' Tilly said with a grin. 'Eliot Slater is *very* easy on the eye.'

'Oh, puh-lease.' Claire rolled her eyes in response. 'Yes, he's nice enough. He's good with the parents.' And, yes, he was easy on the eye—fair Celtic skin teamed with dark hair and eyes the colour of peridot. 'But at the end of the day he's like every other locum and leaves dead on the dot.'

'And so does every other medic with any sense,' Tilly pointed out. 'Don't judge him too harshly—just because you're a workaholic and spend every second you can on the ward, Claire Thurman, it doesn't mean everyone else has to. He's probably got a life, that's all.'

'I'm not a workaholic. I just happen to like my job. Anyway, I go out with the rest of you, don't I?'

'Only because you know I'd nag you if you didn't,' Tilly said. 'Seriously, I know he's a couple of years younger than you, but maybe a toyboy would do you good.'

Claire laughed. 'Tills, I know you're blissfully married, but not everyone wants the same as you do. So don't get any of your matchmaking ideas, will you?'

'Me?' the nurse practitioner deadpanned.

'Yeah, you, Tilly Mortimer. Like the last time you begged me to go to the theatre with you because Matt didn't like Shakespeare, and you'd already bought the tickets. Except when I turned up, you weren't sitting next to me.'

'It was worth a try. And Robin was a nice bloke.'

'And desperate to get married and have babies. You know that's not for me.' If Claire told the lie often enough, maybe she'd end up believing it.

'You're a paediatrician—a neonatal specialist, to be precise, so don't you dare tell me you hate babies.'

'I don't. I just don't want my own.' Another lie. But, thanks to her ex-husband Paddy kissing more than just the Blarney Stone, Claire couldn't have children of her own, something she hadn't admitted even to her closest friends.

Everyone simply thought she'd divorced Padraig O'Neill for adultery and had picked up the pieces of her life, and was happy concentrating on her career. And she was happy to let them think it.

But today Claire had received a letter from Brigid, her ex-mother-in-law, who still stayed in touch. One of Brigid's warm, happy, chatty letters that usually made Claire smile and pick up the phone. Except this one had contained some news Claire really hadn't wanted to hear—that Paddy had just had a son. Padraig O'Neill junior, a beautiful bouncing nine pounds and with his father's curly dark hair and gorgeous smile.

A son that should have been hers.

A son she'd never have, thanks to her ex-husband.

Claire pushed the thought away. No point in dwelling on might-have-beens. She had to look to the future, not the past. A future with herself as consultant. Senior consultant. Professor of neonatology. That was enough.

It had to be.

'Anyway, he's probably already spoken for.'

'You mean, you don't know?' Tilly raised an eyebrow. 'Isn't it in his file?'

'I was more interested in his work,' Claire said wryly. 'And I'm staying happily single at least until I've got a consultant's post, thank you very much.'

'Firstly, he doesn't *look* married. Secondly, you're practically consultant now—you're acting consultant, and that's near enough in my book. You just need to meet Mr Right. Or Dr Right.'

Claire smiled. 'Thanks, but I'm fine and dandy on my own, Tills. I don't need any complications.'

Eliot had been about to go to the nurses' station when he'd heard his name mentioned and decided it probably wasn't a good time to interrupt. Now, standing in the corridor and hearing Claire's scathing comment, he gritted his teeth. *Like every other locum…leaves dead on the dot.* That really wasn't fair. He'd been working at Ludbury Memorial Hospital for a week and he gave his all when he was in the neonatal unit. But he couldn't blindly disregard his working hours. It wasn't because he was lazy or didn't want to work a single second more than he was paid for, as Claire had implied. It was simply that he knew if his time-keeping wasn't perfect, Fran would leave and everything would collapse around his ears.

He'd become a locum five years ago so he could walk away when he needed to, without letting the team down. But the senior registrar clearly thought he was a lightweight. Eliot burned with the injustice of it. Though if he explained to her now, he'd feel he was pressing the point too hard. Or, worse, whining for sympathy. And didn't they say that eavesdroppers never heard any good of themselves?

He took a deep breath and walked round to the nurses' station.

'Dr Slater.' Claire gave him a very professional smile. 'What can I do for you?'

'I've just updated the notes on Becky Poole if you want to review the file, Dr Thurman,' he said.

'Thank you.' She took the proffered file. 'You're due a break, aren't you?'

That comment about locums still rankled: no way was he going to go off duty for even a second before his shift ended. 'Doesn't matter,' he said.

'Actually, it does,' Claire said, surprising him. 'The special care baby unit's a high-pressure environment, so you need regular breaks to recharge your batteries.' She gave him a half-smile that made his heart rate speed up a notch. 'I don't crack the whip that hard on my staff.'

'Regular dragon is our Claire,' Tilly said with a grin.

Claire pulled a face at her. 'Yeah, right. I have a patient to see. Catch you later.'

'Her bark's worse than her bite,' Tilly told Eliot.

'I didn't think dragons barked,' Eliot said drily.

Tilly chuckled. 'This one does. Seriously, Eliot, don't take any notice if she growls at you. Claire's great. She backs her staff to the hilt—no politics where she's concerned, because the patients come first, last and always. So how long are you with us?'

'Until Kelly comes back,' he said, referring to the doctor he was filling in for while she was on maternity leave. 'Unless… But no. He wasn't going to tempt fate and think up problems. Be positive, he told himself. Fran was going to stay and Ryan was going to be just fine.

Some time later, Eliot was called down to the maternity ward to look at one of the newborns. 'I'm not happy about this little one,' Shannon told him. 'Ricky Peters—he's twenty hours old, a thirty-seven-weeker, weight a shade under six pounds. He's his mum's first baby. No problems in the pregnancy, though she had a bit of a long labour and she needed a ventouse at the end.'

'What was his Apgar score?' Eliot asked. The Apgar score was a way of classifying the baby's condition one minute and five minutes after birth—relating to the baby's breathing, heart rate, colour, muscle tone and reaction to stimulation. A high score usually meant that the baby would be fine.

'Six, at five minutes,' Shannon said.

Not quite as good as Eliot had hoped—he'd really wanted a nine or ten—but not that bad either. 'What are his symptoms?' Eliot asked.

'That's just it. I can't put my finger on it— I just know that something isn't right. He's a bit sleepy, which I know you'd expect in an early baby, but he's not feeding as well as he was earlier.'

Shannon's badge proclaimed she was a senior midwife. Eliot decided to trust her instincts.

'Mum's temperature is up a bit, too,' Shannon said.

A bell rang in the back of Eliot's head. Maternal fever... 'Did she have group B strep during pregnancy?' he asked.

Shannon looked through the notes. 'She wasn't tested, according to this.'

And even if she had been, Eliot knew that the test was unreliable, with a fifty per cent false negative result. 'Let's have a look at him,' Eliot said.

Shannon introduced him to Leona Peters, and Eliot duly admired the baby. 'Well done, you. He's gorgeous,' he said, cuddling the baby.

'My hubby says he looks like a Martian with that pointed head,' Leona said wryly.

'So do all ventouse babies—but it doesn't last. His head'll be back to normal before you know it,' Eliot reassured her. 'Right, then, little one, let's see how you're doing.' The baby's heart rate was a bit on the high side for Eliot's liking, and the baby was breathing fast and 'grunting' slightly. Ricky was also slightly irritable during the examination, and the warning bell in the back of Eliot's head grew stronger.

'I'd like to do a few tests, Mrs Peters—just to rule out a couple of things that might be brewing,' he said. 'I'd like to take him up to my ward—the neonatal unit—to warm him up a bit.'

Leona looked alarmed. 'Special Care, you mean? How long will he be there?'

'It shouldn't be too long. And you're very welcome to come with him,' Eliot said. He knew it was the ward policy to encourage bonding between parents and babies.

She nodded. 'I wondered if he was coming down with a cold. I feel a bit groggy at the moment, and there's been a filthy summer cold going round at home.'

'Could be.' It could also be something a lot more serious, but Eliot decided not to worry her just yet. 'If it is a virus, it'd be handy to know what it is, so I'll ask Shannon to do a couple of tests on you before you come up, if that's all right.'

He wrapped the baby gently in a blanket. 'Have you got a spare hat, Shannon, and some oxygen to keep him going until I'm upstairs? And could you ring up to Tilly to tell her to expect us?'

'Sure.' Shannon returned a couple of minutes later with the oxygen and a hat. 'Could I ask you to give Mrs Peters a swab, please?' he asked. Roughly one in a thousand babies were born with a group B streptococcal infection, and the numbers were increasing. He lowered his voice slightly. 'I'm a bit concerned about GBS, so I'd like a high vaginal swab, please.'

'Rightio,' Shannon said. 'I'll bring Leona up to you when we've finished down here.'

'Thanks.' He smiled at her and took Ricky up to the neonatal unit.

'Tilly said you had a suspected GBS,' Claire said, coming over to the cubicle just as Eliot settled the baby into the cot.

Eliot nodded. 'He's lethargic, he's not feeding properly—even though the first couple of times at the breast were fine—his heart rate's a bit on the high side, he's grunting and his temperature's up. I know it could be RDS—' RDS, or respiratory distress syndrome, was common in early babies '—but at this stage it's too early to tell if it's that or something else. The mum's got a temperature, too.'

'What's his blood pressure?'

Eliot checked. 'Low. And his breathing's fast. I've asked Shannon on Maternity to give the mum a swab for group B strep—there weren't any indications in the notes.'

'Three out of ten pregnant women have group B strep without any symptoms, and the only reliable test is the enrichment culture method—which isn't widely available,' Claire said. 'So if there weren't any indications to give her antibiotics in labour, the baby could have picked it up as he came through the birth canal. I take it that it was a normal delivery, not a section?'

'Ventouse,' Eliot said. 'So I don't want to take any chances. If it is group B strep, time isn't on our side. I'll get bloods done, a lumbar puncture and an X-ray, but I don't want to wait for a culture. I think we should start him on antibiotics now. Penicillin for group B strep and gentamycin in case it's pneumococcus.'

Claire nodded. Sepsis could suddenly become overwhelming in tiny babies, and if the sepsis was untreated there was a fifty per cent risk of the baby dying. If the lumbar puncture results were clear, they could discontinue antibiotics in forty-eight hours. 'We need to keep a really close eye on him in the next two days in case it turns into pneumonia or meningitis. Is the mum coming up?'

'When she's had her swab.'

'Good. Do you want me to talk to her about the possibility of group B strep?' Claire asked.

'No, I'll do it,' Eliot said. 'But if you're offering…'

'You want me to do the lumbar puncture?' Claire guessed.

He nodded. 'I really hate doing them.'

Claire brushed the backs of her fingers against the baby's cheek. 'I'll try not to hurt you, little one. I'll get the pack while you sort out the bloods,' she said.

Weird, Eliot thought as he took the blood samples and labelled them carefully. Although he'd spent a week on the ward, it felt as if they'd worked together for years. It was as if she could read his mind. Or maybe it was just as Tilly had said: Claire was a good doctor. She knew her job so well that of course she could second-guess everything he was going to say. Just as she would with any other SHO.

'Can you hold him in position for me?' Claire asked.

'Sure.' Gently, Eliot manoeuvred the baby into position.

'Thanks.' Claire counted down to the space between the third and fourth vertebrae and cleaned the area thoroughly. Then she gave the baby a local anaesthetic, waited a couple of minutes for the lignocaine to numb his back, then took the sample of cerebrospinal fluid. 'All done, littlie,' she said softly to the baby. She capped the needle and put a fresh sterile swab over the puncture, pressing on the area to stop the flow of fluid, then applied a spray dressing.

'There you go,' she said, stroking the baby's arm. 'We'll have your mum up to see you any second now. And Eliot's going to sort out your temperature and make it easier for you to breathe.'

She'd used his first name almost unconsciously, and Eliot was shocked by the pleasure that glowed through him. No. He couldn't start thinking like that about Claire Thurman. She might be single, but nothing could happen between them. Number one, she was his boss. Number two, and most importantly, he had to put Ryan first. Number three, Claire had made it very clear she wasn't looking for marriage and babies—if she didn't want her own child, she certainly wouldn't want to take on someone else's.

This relationship was going to be professional only, he told himself. And he wasn't going to start thinking about her chestnut hair, how it might look if he loosened it from the stern French pleat and let it run through his fingers. He wasn't going to start thinking about what colour her dark eyes would be when she'd just been kissed. And he definitely wasn't going to start thinking about her beautifully shaped mouth…

'So you'll explain to the mum that we're going to feed him through a line?'

Eliot pulled himself together with difficulty. 'And that if it is group B strep, he'll need to be in for ten days or so.'

'Right. I'll get this lot off to the lab, then.' She swiftly measured six drops of spinal fluid into three sample bottles and labelled them.

Just as Claire was about to leave, Shannon Hooper brought Leona Peters up in a wheel-chair.

'Is he all right?' Leona asked, visibly pan-icking.

'He'll be fine. He's having a bit of a rough ride at the moment, but we're keeping him comfortable while we find out what the bug is,' Claire said. 'I'm Claire Thurman, the se-nior registrar on the neonatal unit. I believe you've already met Dr Slater, who's looking after Ricky for you.'

'Yes.' Leona's face was pinched with strain.

'It can be a bit scary up here, with all the wires and equipment,' Claire said, 'but try not to worry. It's there so we can make sure he gets enough oxygen and his temperature's un-der control. I'm taking these samples off to the lab, and Dr Slater will tell you more about what's happening.'

Eliot smiled reassuringly at Leona. 'We think he might have something called group B streptococcus. It's a bacterium that lives in just about everyone's body at some point, usually without any effects, but babies can't cope very well with it—especially if they're a bit early. We've put Ricky on some antibiotics, and he's going to find it very hard to feed for the next day or so—he'll be tired because he's found it a bit difficult to breathe—but we're going to give him some food through a line in his arm until he's up to feeding again, and he'll be able to take some breast milk from you later.'

'Can I touch him?' Leona asked.

'Of course you can. Hold his hand, stroke him, talk to him—he'll know you're here and it will help him.'

'How long will he be in here?'

'It depends how he responds to the antibiotics,' Eliot said. 'Probably ten days or so.' Unless there was a complication such as meningitis, when it would be another three or four days. 'It's probably best to take it day by day for now.'

'Is he going to die?' Leona asked, her face crumpling.

'We've caught the bug early, so he's got a much better chance than if we'd left it,' Eliot said. 'There's a ninety per cent chance he'll be fine. Those are pretty good odds.' Though it still meant there was a ten per cent chance they might lose him... 'How are you feeling?'

'Rotten,' she admitted. 'I thought when you had a baby it was like being a bride—you're meant to be all sparkling and happy and radiant. But...' She shook her head. 'All this. It just doesn't seem real.'

'Hey. Don't be too tough on yourself. Having a baby's hard work. What they don't tell you is that afterwards you just feel shattered and want a good sleep. Plus your hormones are settling down and your milk's coming in, so you'll feel all over the place for a couple of days. Trust me. This time next week, you'll wonder what all the fuss was about.'

'Really?'

'Really.' Though it hadn't quite worked like that for Malandra. He suppressed the thought rapidly. Hopefully Ricky wouldn't have to go through what Ryan had five years ago.

Leona gave him a watery smile. 'Maybe.'

'Hey. Come and give your son a cuddle—that'll help you feel better.' He wheeled Leona next to the incubator. 'Put your hand through the porthole here and let him hold your finger.'

'He's holding on,' Leona said, sounding amazed.

'We're keeping a close eye on him, and all these machines are just helping us check his temperature, how much oxygen is in his blood, how fast his heart's beating and how fast he's breathing. I'll introduce you to the nurse who'll be looking after him on this shift,' Eliot said, 'and she'll be able to tell you where the phone is, where the vending machine is and that sort of thing.'

'Intensive care. It sounds so…' Leona's face crumpled; she covered her face with her hands and started to sob.

'It sounds scary, I know, but he's in the best possible hands,' Eliot soothed. 'Try not to worry. Really. We know how precious he is to you, and we'll take the best possible care of him.'

Leona sobbed harder, and Eliot patted her shoulder, wishing he could comfort her and knowing that if he didn't leave soon, he'd be late and…

Hell. He was damned if he did, damned if he didn't. This was definitely one of those days when he wished he'd suppressed his love of medicine and found himself a nice steady administrative job somewhere, where his hours would be regular and he could take work home to make up for not staying late at the office.

If only Tilly hadn't said it. *Easy on the eye... Maybe a toyboy would do you good...*

No. Claire was going to stick to her plan: no relationships until she made consultant. And then whoever she married would have to accept that her career came first and children wouldn't even be an issue.

And yet... Damn. She kept seeing Eliot Slater in her mind's eye. The kindness on his face as he explained procedures to a distraught parent. The gentleness in his eyes as he treated a tiny baby. Worse, her mind supplied other images. His pupils widening as he looked at her. Those beautiful green eyes darkening with passion. His mouth parting as it lowered to—

No. This wasn't fair. Why couldn't she have had a female locum? Or a man who was silver-haired, the favourite-uncle type? But, no, she got a man two years younger than she was, with film-star good looks. Dark curly hair that he kept cut short and tamed for work, fair skin, beautiful green eyes and a mouth that promised a mixture of passion and vulnerability.

But, as she'd said to Tilly, Eliot Slater was probably already involved. She couldn't remember what it had said on his file, but even if he wasn't spoken for, she had a feeling that Eliot had his own ghosts to deal with. According to his résumé, he was thirty. By now, she'd have expected him to be a registrar. But he was still a senior house officer, and he worked as a locum. A locum who only did day shifts. Maybe he was looking after an elderly parent and had to fit in work around day care?

But that was none of her business. She wasn't going to get involved. All she had to worry about was whether Eliot Slater did his job properly. And so far he was doing just fine. He'd picked up a case of potential sepsis—and as they'd caught it early enough, little Ricky Peters stood a good chance.

Eventually Leona stopped crying, and Eliot mopped up her tears and called her husband to explain the news. He was just about to leave the ward when he heard Claire's voice. 'Can I have a quick word, Dr Slater?'

As long as it *was* quick. 'Sure,' he said, willing himself not to look at his watch.

'I just wanted to say thanks. You did a good job with Ricky Peters,' Claire said.

Praise indeed from Claire Thurman...but her face said the rest of it for her.

Eliot couldn't stop himself. 'For a locum, you mean.'

She frowned. 'I'm not with you.'

'I overheard you talking to Tilly earlier.'

'Oh.' Her face was impassive. 'Well, you do leave dead on the dot. And you don't do nights.'

He nearly said, 'Locum's privilege,' but stopped himself just in time. He needed Claire on his side, not against him. 'I'm committed to my job, Dr Thurman. While I'm on duty, I'll give a hundred per cent. But I can't work longer hours, for personal reasons.'

Claire waited, as if giving him time to explain, but Eliot had no intention of doing that. He didn't want pity from anyone. And he particularly didn't want pity from Claire.

Though he wouldn't allow himself to speculate about what exactly he *did* want from her. It was way too dangerous.

'See you tomorrow,' he said, and walked out of the door.

CHAPTER TWO

OH, GREAT. He *would* have to get stuck in a traffic jam. Eliot rang home and the answering-machine kicked in. He stifled the panic that lurched in his stomach. Of course Fran hadn't left Ryan on his own. She wasn't Malandra. She'd wait until he got home. Probably she hadn't heard the phone, or she was busy cooking Ryan's tea or something.

The message ended with a long beep, and Eliot gabbled his message. 'It's me—I'm on my way but I'm stuck in traffic. I'll be back as soon as I can.'

By the time he finally walked through the front door, he could feel his blood pressure simmering. He took a deep breath and reminded himself to stay calm, for Ryan's sake.

Ryan was in front of the TV, half watching a cartoon and half concentrating on a complex model of a robot that he'd made from K'nex, snapping the rods and links together as if he instinctively knew the right pattern. Eliot al-

26

ways marvelled at how his son could produce an intricate three-dimensional jet or helicopter with a moving rotor in such a short space of time.

'Hi, son.'

Ryan didn't look up, he just muttered, 'Hi, Dad,' the way he usually did. Eliot suppressed the yearning to have his son run to him and hug him and look into his eyes and laugh. *Hello, Dad. I missed you. I love you.* Followed by lots of chattering about what happened at school today, what he'd been doing with Fran, what he wanted to do this evening.

Dream on, Eliot told himself savagely. You know that's not going to happen. And it's not his fault or yours. It's just the way it is and you have to live with it.

'Fran? I'm back.'

Fran appeared at the kitchen doorway. 'I was just making Ryan's tea,' she said. 'Chicken nuggets, chips and spaghetti.'

Not exactly the best nutrition in the world, Eliot knew—but he'd learned the hard way not to make food into a battleground. Nowadays he gave Ryan what he knew the seven-year-old would eat, and tried to sneak fruit and vegetables into his son when he could. 'Thanks, Fran. I owe you an extra hour. Plus overtime,' he added guiltily.

She didn't look even remotely mollified. 'You said you'd be home by half past.'

'I know. And I would have been, but I got stuck in traffic.' Eliot sighed. 'I *am* trying, Fran.'

'I've got a life, you know. I'm never going to be ready for my date tonight.'

'I'm sorry.'

'Sorry is as sorry does.'

Eliot almost snapped back at her—but thought better of it at the last moment. If he didn't keep Fran sweet, she'd leave. And that would be a disaster. It had taken him four months to find Fran. Four months of Ryan being unsettled at the constant changes in his child care, four months of interviews and wondering if he'd ever find the right person to look after his child between school and his job, four months when he'd had to stop working and he'd lived on home-made vegetable soup and toast because it was cheap.

'Look—have a drink or what have you on me tonight,' he said, taking a note from his wallet.

'Ta.' Fran pocketed it swiftly. 'The spaghetti's in the microwave and the nuggets and chips are in the oven. They'll be ready in ten minutes. See you tomorrow.' She paused at the living-room doorway. 'Bye, Ryan.'

Ryan didn't acknowledge his childminder, simply continued with his model-making. Two others were neatly lined up and there was a space next to them ready for the one he was making now.

'Tea's in ten minutes,' Eliot told him.

'Mmm,' was the response. Ryan was focused completely on his model.

Ten minutes later, they were sitting at the dining-room table. Eliot had managed to find the right knife and fork, made sure none of the three types of food touched any of the others and were on the right plate, and he'd filled Ryan's mug with milk to precisely one centimetre from the top.

His thanks were simply that Ryan ate without fuss or comment. Apart from once, when he looked at his father's sandwich. 'Fran didn't get you any bacon.'

'That's OK. Tuna salad's cool.' Actually, Eliot was sick to the back teeth of bacon sandwiches. Maybe he was pandering to Ryan's little routines too much. The psychologist would tell him he had to fight more battles. Though Eliot didn't want to fight his son. He only wanted to love him.

'What happened at school today?'

'Maths.'

Amazing how Ryan could answer an open question with a closed statement. Eliot tried again. 'What was the best thing today?'

'I had strawberries in my lunch.'

He knew that was as much as he was going to get. The same as he'd heard every other school day for the last month. Just for once Eliot longed to hear his son say he'd played football or found a butterfly or learned a new song. But he'd find out those sorts of things at the monthly review meetings with Ryan's teacher and support assistant.

Eliot let his son eat the rest of his meal in silence.

'Can I go on the computer now?' Ryan asked.

'Half an hour. When you've done your homework.'

'It's just reading.'

'OK. How about half an hour on the computer, bath, then you read to me?' It was a risk, changing his routine, but for once Ryan didn't seem to mind.

'OK, Dad.'

Ryan was gone, and within seconds Eliot heard the computer booting up. He finished his sandwich and then cleared up in the kitchen. Bathtime was the highlight of his day—playing submarines with his son, though the routine never varied and Ryan always sank Eliot's ships in the exact same order.

Milk, teeth and story. Ryan read his book fluently, and Eliot gave him a gold star, sticking it like a medal on his pyjamas. 'Well done. That's for reading expressive dialogue.' Ryan had clearly been working hard on expression with his support assistant at school.

'Thanks, Dad.'

'Sleep well.' Eliot hugged him. 'I love you.'

As always, Ryan's face had a slightly worried look and his eyes slid away, not meeting his father's. Eliot squashed his inward sigh. He knew that Ryan loved him; the little boy just wasn't comfortable saying so. Facts, fine—emotions, not.

'See you in the morning. Light off in half an hour, OK?'

'All right. 'Night, Dad.'

Ryan was already deep in a scientific text-book before Eliot even left the room. Wearily, Eliot walked downstairs and tried to keep a certain pair of dark eyes out of his head—with very little success.

This wasn't fair. He didn't stand a snow-flake in hell's chance with her. *Babies… I just don't want my own.* Someone else's child—a child who was a little different, to say the least—would be even more of a no-no. So why couldn't he stop thinking about Claire Thurman?

'She's been waiting for you. Pacing up and down,' Vi said with a grin. 'According to mad-am here, you're half an hour late.'

Bess barked and wagged her tail.

Claire ruffled the golden retriever's ears. 'Sneak. Now your other mum'll be on at me for putting in too many hours at the hospital.'

'I know you want to get on, love, but there's life outside work,' Vi said.

'And mine suits me perfectly. Half-shares in the best dog in the world, a good run each night and going out with friends at the week-end.'

'Hmm.'

Claire knew exactly what Vi's murmur meant. *You need a husband and a family.* But she also knew her life wasn't going to turn out that way. And she was happy enough. She'd come to terms with what had happened—she'd even forgiven Paddy for it.

Though not quite enough to accept Brigid's invitation to Paddy junior's christening.

'Come on, you. Time for your run,' Claire said, clipping Bess's lead to her collar.

'And I'll have the kettle on for when you get back,' Vi said.

'Thanks, Vi.'

Five minutes of a steady pace, with Bess loping beside her, was enough to restore Claire's equilibrium. And that was when the guilt kicked in. The look on Eliot's face when she'd suggested that he take a break... He'd clearly overheard what she'd said to Tilly. And maybe she had been a bit harsh. Brigid's letter had unsettled her, but she really shouldn't have taken it out on him.

Then she remembered the rest of the conversation and her face turned bright red. Oh, no. If he'd heard Tilly trying to pair him off with Claire... Embarrassing. As well as an apology tomorrow, she'd explain to him that Tilly was a newlywed and wanted to pair off all the unattached people she knew—it wasn't anything personal.

Personal. Now that was a dangerous word to think in the same thought as Eliot Slater.

'Oh, get a grip,' she said aloud. 'He's probably attached and, even if he isn't, he wouldn't be interested in me. I'm practically his boss, I'm older than he is and I don't do relationships anyway.' That decided, she upped the pace until she reached the park.

Claire didn't see Eliot the next morning, but assumed he was as busy with patients as she was. When she finally took a break for lunch, she grabbed a glass of freshly squeezed orange juice, a plate of chicken salad and a nectarine. Just as she paid she spotted him at a corner table in the cafeteria. Now was as good a time as any to apologise. Better, in fact, because at least it was on neutral ground rather than on the ward.

'Mind if I join you?'

Eliot glanced up from the journal he'd been reading, looking surprised. 'Sorry?'

Well, obviously he'd been concentrating—but Claire still felt her face grow hot, and was annoyed at herself. She wasn't going to lose her cool for anyone. 'Mind if I join you?' she repeated.

'No, feel free.'

'Great.' She plonked her tray opposite him and sat down. 'I'm glad I've caught you. I wanted to apologise for yesterday.'

He frowned. 'Apologise?'

'I was a bit snappy with you. Bad day.'

'Right.'

'I'm not normally like that. Well, not unless I'm unhappy with a patient's care—then, I growl a lot,' she added with a grin. 'How are you settling in?'

'Fine. I like the unit—everyone's friendly and it seems like a well-oiled machine.'

'They're a nice bunch,' Claire said. 'As well as being the best medics in the hospital.'

'Not that you're biased, of course.'

She hadn't expected that. So far, he'd been serious whenever he'd spoken to her. A dry sense of humour and a twinkle in those green eyes…now, that was dangerous. And looking at his mouth instead of his eyes was a very big mistake—because his mouth was perfect. Wide, generous and with a killer smile. The sort of mouth she could imagine against hers. Exploring her body. Making her—

No. Even if he was free, it couldn't work. He'd probably want a family, in time, and she couldn't do that. Best not to start something that could only end in tears. It took a huge effort, but she managed to turn the conversation back to work and their patients.

Something had spooked her, Eliot thought. But he couldn't think of anything he'd said that might have upset her. All he knew was that that beautiful grin—the one that had made his pulse rocket—had disappeared and she was back to being the brisk, chirpy professional he'd seen on the ward.

Professional was the only relationship they could have anyway. He knew that. He'd spent most of a sleepless night telling himself that. If it came to a choice between Claire and Ryan, there was no contest. He wouldn't choose *anyone* over Ryan. But if only he could have had both…

Later that afternoon, Eliot looked at the baby in front of him and frowned. He had a nasty feeling about this. The baby had been born a few weeks early and the vernix—the waxy substance that protected the baby's skin from the amniotic fluid in the womb—wasn't the usual white colour: it was yellow. The baby's skin was definitely yellow, too. And there was a definite abdominal mass which felt to him as if the spleen and the liver were both swollen, a condition known as hepatosplenomegaly. One look at the notes confirmed his suspicions.

'Got a moment, please, Claire?'

'Sure.' She looked up from her notes. 'Problem?'

He handed her the notes.

She sucked her teeth. 'Are you thinking rhesus haemolytic disease?'

'Looks like it. Mum's rhesus negative, the baby's jaundiced and there was definite hepatosplenomegaly when I examined him.'

'Better get the cord blood tested for blood group and the Coombs test, plus haemoglobin and bilirubin levels.' The first two tests would confirm the diagnosis of rhesus haemolytic disease, and the second two would tell them how serious the condition was. Claire shook her head. 'How on earth was this missed? Rhesus-negative mums are supposed to be tested for D antibodies at booking, twenty-eight weeks and thirty-four weeks. She could have had anti-D injections and the baby would have been fine.'

'First baby, and she was a bit slapdash about going to the clinic.' He coughed. 'Apparently the dad's rhesus negative as well.'

Claire frowned. 'If the mum's blood group is negative and the baby's blood group is positive, the dad's must be positive, too.' Then she bit her lip. 'Ah. This might get messy,' she said softly. 'Want a hand?'

'Please. She might tell you a bit more than she told me.'

'Claire the dragon, scaring her into it, you mean?' she teased.

'Claire the woman,' he said. Then wished he hadn't when she blushed. Very prettily.

Because again it made him want to know what she looked like when she'd just been thoroughly kissed. By him. 'Girl power,' he said hastily.

'Right.' She didn't say anything, but he had a nasty feeling she'd been able to read his mind. The problem was, he couldn't read hers. Claire was unattached—Tilly had told him that much—but why? Was it that she'd concentrated on her career and hadn't met the right man yet?

Well, he wasn't the right man for her either. Because he came as a package, the kind of package that very few women would be interested in taking on.

'Estée, this is Claire Thurman, our senior registrar and acting consultant,' he said.

'What's wrong with Miles?' Estée asked, her face pinched and drawn.

'We're doing some blood tests to find out, but Eliot thinks it's rhesus haemolytic disease. If he's right...' Claire took a swift look at the baby '...and I'm pretty sure he is, then we can help Miles and he'll be fine.'

'What's rhesus haemolytic disease?' Estée asked.

'People's blood type is grouped into A, AB, B or O, and then it's either rhesus positive or negative. When you're pregnant, some of the baby's red blood cells leak into your system,' Claire explained. 'That's perfectly normal and doesn't usually matter at all—but if your blood group is rhesus negative and your baby's blood group is rhesus positive, the leak of blood into your system makes your body produce anti-bodies. This won't affect you at all, but it might affect your baby in any future pregnancies, because if any future baby is rhesus positive, the tiniest leak of blood will make your body produce antibodies, which can cross the placenta and attack the baby's red blood cells. The baby's red blood cells change in shape and don't last for as long as they should do, so the baby can become very anaemic and jaundiced. If the baby's really badly affected, it might turn into a condition known as hydrops fe-talis—meaning that the baby's tissues are very swollen—and there's a much greater risk of stillbirth. So that's why, if we knew you're rhesus negative, we'd give you an injection of something called anti-D, which stops your body producing these antibodies.'

Estée bit her lip. 'Right.'

'It doesn't usually affect first babies,' Claire said, 'unless you've had a bit of bleeding during your pregnancy, or a threatened miscarriage, or a test such as an amniocentesis. And your midwife really should have tested your blood when she booked you in, plus twice more in later pregnancy.'

'I'm not good with needles,' Estée said. She wrinkled her nose. 'It's my fault. She said she needed to do it but I kept saying I'd do it next time.'

Claire sat next to Estée and held her hand. 'Except then you missed your appointments,' she said gently. 'Estée, you took a risk with yourself as well as your baby. Antenatal appointments are a way of letting your midwife check that you're OK during your pregnancy and not developing any conditions such as pre-eclampsia, which could make you or your baby very ill.'

'But I was really well—I was hardly even sick! I didn't show until nearly six months...' Estée chewed her lip again. 'He will be all right, won't he?'

'We'll do our best. If it is rhesus haemolytic disease, we can give him a transfusion which will take some of the bilirubin out of his blood—that's the chemical that's turning him yellow—and help increase his red blood cells, which will get rid of the anaemia. We can also give him light treatment. That just means putting him under a bank of lights which will help with the jaundice.'

'So he's not going to die?'

'Not if I can help it.' Claire squeezed her hand. 'But I do need to know a couple of things, Estée. Things that will stay totally confidential, but that will help us to help Miles.'

Estée thought for a moment. 'All right.'

'But before we talk, I need a blood sample. I promise you, you're not going to feel a thing.'

'She's brilliant,' Eliot said. 'If she can take blood from tiny, fragile premature babies without hurting them, just think how easy it'll be for you.'

'I hate needles,' Estée said.

'Then turn and talk to Eliot,' Claire suggested. 'Tell him all about the nursery you've got planned for Miles.'

Eliot came to sit by the other side of Estée's bed. 'This is the bit I like. Holding the hand of the prettiest mums,' he said. 'It's nearly as good as cuddling a new baby.'

'Oh, men!' Estée said.

Claire gave Eliot the thumbs-up sign.

'So, what colours are you using?'

'Yellow,' Estée said. 'With teddy bears. I didn't know if it was a boy or a girl, so I wimped out and played safe.'

'Sounds great. Babies love teddies.' He almost swapped confidences and told her that he'd stencilled Ryan's room with teddies, but he managed to bite the words back at the last moment.

'All done,' Claire said, capping the sample.

Estée stared at her in amazement. 'But—I didn't even feel it.'

'I told you so.' Eliot winked at her. 'Claire's the best.'

'Can you sort the tests, please, Eliot?' Claire asked.

He nodded and left the room.

'OK, Estée. Well done for being brave. I hate needles, too,' Claire said. 'So, can you tell me, is Miles your first baby?'

'Yes.'

'You haven't had a miscarriage before?'

'No.'

'Any bleeding in this pregnancy?'

'Just a bit of spotting. My friend said it wasn't anything to worry about so I didn't bother telling my midwife.'

'Right.' The tiny haemorrhage had probably been enough to start the antibodies; in subsequent pregnancies it could take as little as 0.03 ml of the baby's blood to make Estée's body produce the antibodies. 'Do you know your husband's blood group?'

'He's A negative, like me.'

'Right.' Claire took a deep breath. Now for the crunch question. 'I'm sorry to ask you this, Estée, but is there any chance that your husband isn't your baby's father?'

'Oh, God.' Estée's face crumpled and she sobbed. 'Roger mustn't know.' She closed her eyes. 'I found out he'd had an affair with his secretary. I wanted to pay him back, so I had a fling with his best mate one night. Mickey and I were drunk… The worst thing is, it didn't even make me feel better. Then I found out I was pregnant. I was so sure it was Roger's. I mean, me and Mickey…it was only once.'

'Once is all it takes,' Claire said drily. 'If you and Roger are both A negative, Miles should be A negative, too. So Mickey's blood group must be rhesus positive, and Miles must be his baby.'

'What am I going to do? If Roger dumps me because of this… I don't want to be a single mum. I'd never cope. He doesn't even really want kids—so I didn't tell him for weeks and weeks, until it was almost too late to do anything and… Oh, God. What am I going to do?' Estée wailed.

'It'll sort itself out. The first thing to concentrate on is making Miles better,' Claire said. 'Try not to worry. We have people you can talk to here—counsellors who can help you through the problems you might face with your husband. But right now your son needs you on his side. He needs cuddles and for you to talk to him, sing to him, let him know you're here. And as soon as we get the test results back, we'll be able to start treatment.'

'Thank you. I'm sorry for being so wet. It's…'

'You've just had a baby. Your hormones are all over the place, you're worried about your son, and it's perfectly natural.' Claire squeezed her hand again. 'I'll come back and see you as soon as I've got the results. In the meantime, if you need anything, the nurses are here to help.'

'Thank you,' Estée said again.

Ten minutes later, Eliot rapped on her open office door. At her nod, he walked in and closed the door behind him. 'Well?'

'You were right. The baby isn't her husband's. She had a fling to pay him back for cheating on her.' Claire shook her head. 'Marriage is the pits. If people thought about the possible consequences before they had an affair—and I mean *really* thought—they'd never do it. It causes way too much mess and pain.'

It sounded as if she was talking from the heart. She must have been married before, Eliot thought, and he guessed that her marriage had disintegrated after an affair. From what Eliot knew of her, Claire wasn't the type to have a fling—she was way too honest. So she must have been the one to get hurt. No wonder she'd stayed focused on her career.

He couldn't help himself. He took her hand and squeezed it. And then somehow—he really wasn't sure how it had happened—he was holding her. Stroking her hair, hair that was as soft and silky as he'd thought it would be, and he wanted to unpin it, let it fall round her face and soften her professional doctor look.

He was close enough to inhale the fragrance of her skin, a soft, sweet scent that made him want to touch her even more. His cheek was pressed against hers and he could feel her heartbeat—slightly irregular, like his own. She must be as knocked off balance as he was. And he couldn't stop. From nuzzling her cheek, it was only one tiny step to—

'I don't think this is a good idea.'

Her voice was quiet yet firm. Eliot dropped his hands immediately and backed off. Though he couldn't help looking in her eyes, and her eyes definitely weren't giving the same message as her mouth. She'd clearly felt the same spark of awareness that he had.

Except she was a lot more professional in the way she dealt with it.

'I'm sorry. I don't know...' He raked his hand through his hair. 'No. I do know.' He wasn't going to insult her by pretending. He shrugged awkwardly. 'It sounded like you were speaking from experience. And I just wanted to give you a hug.'

'Thanks, but I'm a big girl. I can look after myself,' she said drily, sitting back down at her desk.

It was his turn to flush. She'd made her position very, very clear. 'And I was out of order. Sorry.'

'Don't worry about it. We all act on impulse from time to time.'

'Yeah.' She was giving him a let-out, and he seized it gratefully. 'Call it kid-brother syndrome.'

To his relief, that made her smile. 'I'm the youngest. So I'll have to take your word for that.' She coughed. 'I'll, um, see you when the results are back, then.'

'OK.' He left her office and closed the door behind him. Dismissed, in the nicest possible way. And he'd really, really blown it. Why hadn't he kept his hands to himself?

You know why, a little voice said inside his head. Because she's gorgeous. The kind of woman you've always dreamed of.

Yes. But he couldn't have her.

Ignoring the sour taste in his mouth, he scooped up a set of notes and went to see his tiny patient.

As her office door shut, Claire leaned back in her chair and closed her eyes. Hell, hell, hell. Why had she let her mouth run away with her like that? She'd virtually told Eliot she'd been unhappily married. And when he'd given her a hug—what he'd said had been a kid-brother sort of hug—she'd been so near to embarrassing them both. For a mad moment she'd actually thought about moving her head, letting her lips trail over his. Kissing him. For an even madder moment, she'd thought he'd been about to do the same.

Thank God they hadn't. Because now she knew he thought of her as his big sister; he'd only given her a hug because he'd thought she could do with one.

The problem was, she couldn't reciprocate. She simply couldn't see Eliot Slater as her kid brother. Not now she knew what it felt like, being held by him. And he smelled good, clean and male. And...

Stop right there, Claire Thurman, she told herself. It isn't going to happen. Your relationship's strictly professional. And it's going to stay that way. He's your junior, and you're going to do the big-sister, kid-brother thing, even if it kills you.

When the test results came back, both Claire and Eliot managed to pretend that the near-clinch in her office had never happened. 'Coombs is positive, baby's blood group is A positive, mum's is A negative.' Eliot frowned at the haemoglobin results. 'I think we should do the exchange transfusion now.'

Claire looked at the results and nodded. 'The haemoglobin's too low to wait for the bilirubin levels. Have you done this before?'

'Once.'

'So you want Claire the dragon to put the big bad needle in?' she teased.

'And I'll get the consent form signed,' he offered. 'Deal?'

'Right. I'll get Tilly to do the monitoring.'

He checked his watch. 'An exchange transfusion usually takes about two hours, doesn't it?'

'And you can't stay that long.'

He hated the disappointment in her eyes. But how could he explain that it wasn't her, it wasn't anything to do with what had nearly happened between them in her office, without going into detail about his family circumstances? Detail he didn't want to go into, because he definitely didn't want her pity. 'Sorry,' he muttered.

'No problem.'

'Tills—case conference,' Claire said when they reached the nurses' station. 'We have a little one with rhesus haemolytic disease, and we're going to do an exchange transfusion. Which means, Eliot?'

'It corrects the anaemia and stops the circulatory system being overloaded—at the moment the baby has a normal blood volume but the central venous pressure's too high. We need to use warmed blood—at thirty-seven degrees—cross-matched against the baby's and the mum's blood. The blood we put in will replace the red blood cells which are coated with antibodies—the new blood will be compatible with the mum's serum so the antibodies won't coat the new red blood cells,' Eliot recited. 'Tilly, Claire's going to do the cannula in the umbilical artery and vein, and we're going to remove the blood in five-mil aliquots from the artery and replace it through continuous infusion into the vein, so there's less risk of the baby's blood pressure fluctuating. The baby may need some pain relief and we need to watch for rebound of the bilirubin serum level.'

Claire nodded. 'OK, you've passed your viva.' She gave him what she hoped was a big-sister grin. 'Tills, we want to monitor Miles's ECG, his Us and Es, bilirubin, glucose—you know there's a risk of rebound hypoglycaemia after the transfusion—and calcium.'

'OK. And are we doing phototherapy after that?'

'Yes. The usual—keep him uncovered as much as possible, keep an eye on his temperature and fluid loss and keep checking the eye shields to make sure they're not irritating his eyes,' Claire confirmed.

'And pinch a surgeon's mask to use as a mini-nappy to protect his gonads from chromatic radiation damage,' Tilly added.

'Why don't we use a phototherapy blanket?' Eliot asked, referring to the fibre-optic filaments which carried a high-intensity halogen light source, woven into a pad which the baby could lie on. 'Then he wouldn't need an eye shield, and it'll be easier for Estée to care for him.'

'We don't have any,' Claire told him. 'We're fundraising at the moment. So if you want to buy some raffle tickets...'

He rolled his eyes. 'OK, OK. Message received and understood.'

'And you're a doctor, so there's a minimum purchase level of ten tickets,' Tilly added.

'I think I'll go and get that consent form signed, before you two get too carried away,' Eliot said with a grin.

'Like I said. He's lovely,' Tilly muttered to Claire when Eliot had gone. 'He'd be good for you.'

'Like I said, it's not going to happen,' Claire muttered back.

If only...

CHAPTER THREE

CLAIRE managed to keep up the 'big sister' act for nearly a week. And then she was heading to her office to write up a patient's notes when she saw a small boy wandering around the ward.

'Hello. Are you lost?' she asked.

He stared at the floor. 'I can't find my dad.'

Claire definitely hadn't seen the boy before. But there was an outside chance he'd visited a younger sibling on the ward when she'd been off duty. 'I'll help you find him. My name's Claire and I'm a doctor here. What's your name?'

'Ryan.'

'Can you tell me your baby brother or sister's name, Ryan?'

He shook his head, still staring at the floor.

Maybe he'd wandered in here from another ward. Or maybe... Something about him reminded her of her godson, Jed. 'Is your baby brother or sister here, sweetheart?' she asked gently.

Again, Ryan shook his head.

'Is your mum or dad a patient here?'

'Dad's a doctor.'

He looked up and in that brief second Claire realised who the boy was. Ryan's eyes were a deep cornflower blue and his hair was mid-brown, but his mouth was identical to a mouth she hadn't been able to get out of her head. Eliot's. 'Is your dad's name Eliot?' she asked carefully.

'Yes.'

Her heart clenched. Eliot had a child. Eliot was *married*. So either he really had meant it about the kid-brother thing, and she'd nearly made a colossal fool of herself, or... Oh, no. He couldn't be another Paddy. He couldn't have been a married man trying to schmooze her just when she'd been saying how affairs wrecked lives. No. He was too nice for that— wasn't he? And Tilly, who had a radar for that sort of thing, had pronounced him unat-tached...

But maybe they'd both been wrong.

She took a deep breath. 'OK, Ryan. Your dad's seeing a patient at the moment. Would you like to come and sit in my office and wait for him?'

'I want Dad.'

'I know, sweetheart, but right now he's with a tiny baby who's very ill. I'll get him for you, but you can't come with me in case you have any germs.'

'Because it's a sterile environment and bacteria multiply rapidly.'

That one had come straight from left field—certainly not what she'd expected from a child this young. But, then again, maybe he'd heard Eliot talk about his job at home. 'I'm impressed,' she said. 'Are you going to be a doctor like your dad when you grow up?'

'No.'

Well, that was her fault for asking a closed question. She thought of Jed again. 'How old are you, Ryan?'

'Seven.'

'Do you like dinosaurs?'

Another flash of those beautiful eyes. 'Yes.'

'I've got some in my office. Do you want to see them while I get your dad?'

'Yes, please.'

'Would you like a drink?'

'Yes, please.'

'What would you like?'

'Milk, please.'

'OK. Come this way.'

'It's the third door on the right,' he said, surprising her. 'I saw it on the map.'

'How did you get here, Ryan?'

'On the bus. Number 17 bus, four stops. Change to a number 20 bus to the hospital. There's always a map of a hospital in Reception. This is the fourth floor, and all the wards on this floor start with D because D's the fourth letter of the alphabet.'

Ryan was definitely like Jed: hated small talk, but could hold forth for hours on subjects that interested him. Facts and figures, maps and dinosaurs, sea creatures. She'd bet good money that Ryan loved trains, robots and astronomy, too. 'Well done, you. We're going to stop by the nurses' kitchen on the way to get you some milk.'

'Thank you.'

Polite, quiet and that steadfast refusal to make eye contact for more than a second. He gave information rather than having a proper conversation, and she had a feeling that Ryan would be a stickler for routine. Typical of a child with Asperger's syndrome.

Which explained why Eliot worked the shifts he did, and why he hadn't wanted to be late. But why hadn't he told her himself? Was she that much of a dragon?

'You should pour it with your right hand,' Ryan remarked when she took the milk carton from the fridge.

'Sorry, Ryan. I'm left-handed. If I pour it with my right, I'll spill it everywhere.'

There was a nasty pause while the little boy digested the information. Then he shrugged. 'OK.'

'Tell me when to stop.' If her suspicions were right, Ryan would be as particular as Jed about how much milk he had in a cup.

'Stop,' he said solemnly when the liquid was one centimetre below the brim.

'Rightio. We'll go to my office and get the dinosaurs, and then I'll fetch your dad.'

'You've got a shark screensaver,' he said immediately when they walked into her office.

'It was my birthday present from my god-son,' she said.

'It's cool.'

'I like it, too.' She rummaged in her desk and found the collection of dinosaurs, plus the set of cards she'd bought for Jed that contained facts and figures about various dinosaurs. 'This game's better for two or more people but you can play it on your own, against yourself, if you like. Now, are you OK to stay here while I get your dad?'

'Yes.'

'If you need anything before we get back, just go to the nurses' station and ask for Tilly.'

'Tilly,' he repeated dutifully.

'I won't be long.' She smiled, left and went to find Eliot in one of the side rooms. 'Can I have a quick word, Dr Slater?'

Eliot looked up from his patient, surprised by her formality. 'Of course.' He followed her outside the room.

'You have a visitor in my office,' she said coolly. 'Name of Ryan Slater.'

Panic gripped him, oozing out of every pore. What was his son doing here? Was he hurt?

And why hadn't Claire mentioned Fran? Eliot forced himself to calm down. 'Is he all right?'

'He's fine. Right now he's looking at my dinosaur cards. I've given him some milk. He wants you, so I'll finish off here.'

'Thanks.' Eliot bit his lip. 'Look, I hope he—'

Clearly his worries were written all over his face, because she cut in, 'He's been no trouble at all.'

'Thanks for looking after him. Um, I'm sorry about this.'

'Not a problem.'

It was, by the look on her face. A big problem. But he'd have to deal with that later—his priority right now was Ryan.

He almost ran to Claire's office, and could have wept when he saw that Ryan was on his own. Had Fran got fed up with waiting and dropped him off at the hospital? 'Ryan! Are you all right?'

'Hi, Dad.' Ryan was acting as if it was nothing out of the usual for him to be sitting in Eliot's boss's office. 'Look, Claire's got these dinosaur cards. It's a game. You have to—'

'Ryan,' Eliot cut in, 'what's happened?'

'I had some milk.'

Specific. He had to remember to ask *specific* questions. Ryan dealt in pure logic. 'Where's Fran?'

'At home with Jon.'

'Who's Jon?'

Ryan shrugged.

Her boyfriend. He must be Fran's boyfriend. 'Does she know you're here?'

'No.'

Then why the hell hadn't Fran phoned him to let him know Ryan was missing?

'How did you get here?'

'Number 17 bus. Four stops, change to number 20 bus to here,' Ryan recited. 'This is the fourth floor—'

'Didn't the bus drivers ask you where your mummy and daddy were?' Eliot cut in.

Ryan shrugged. 'I gave them the right money for my ticket.'

He would. Ryan was excellent with money—he'd grasped the concept much quicker than his classmates, and his maths skills were way ahead of his age. Then a nasty thought hit Eliot. 'Where did you get the money?'

'I took Fran's purse.'

Eliot scooped up his son and sat down with Ryan firmly on his lap. Ryan wriggled, clearly uncomfortable with the close contact. 'Ryan, sweetheart, you really can't just take money from people and get on the bus.'

'But I just did,' Ryan pointed out logically.

'OK. It's something you're not *supposed* to do. Number one, you don't take things without asking and, number two, you always tell someone if you want to go somewhere.' He paused. 'What was Fran doing?'

'Giggling. Jon was taking her clothes off.'

That explained a lot, Eliot thought grimly. 'Has this—has Fran brought Jon to our house before?'

'Yes.'

'A lot?'

'Most days.'

Eliot kept his temper, with difficulty. It wasn't Ryan's fault. But he was angry with Fran—angrier than he'd ever been in his life. To think he'd trusted her with his precious son, and she'd been snippy over him being late when all the time she'd been neglecting Ryan and canoodling with her boyfriend… God only knew what Ryan had seen. His mouth tightened. 'What do you do when Jon's there?'

'Make models, watch telly. But I couldn't find the remote control and Fran told me to go away. So I came to see you.'

'I see.'

'Did I do wrong?' Ryan looked anxious.

'No, sweetheart. You were right to tell me. I'll make it all better again.' Somehow. Maybe the school knew someone who could step in to help—just until he found another childminder. One who, this time, would look after Ryan properly. Who wouldn't pull the wool over his eyes. And he'd check every single reference face to face. Twice.

'Can you stay here for just a moment while I have a word with Claire?'

'Yes, Dad. I know I'm not allowed to go near the babies in case I give them germs.'

'Good boy.' Eliot dropped a kiss on the top of his son's head. 'I'll be back in less than five minutes.'

Remembering her formality with him a few minutes before, he didn't quite dare use her first name. 'Dr Thurman? May I have a word, please?'

'Sure. I'm done here anyway.' She joined him in the corridor.

'I'm sorry to ask, but may I leave early? I have a...' No. He wasn't going to dump his problems on her. It wasn't fair. 'I have a personal problem that needs sorting out.'

'Whatever.'

Brisk, professional. But there was a hint of disappointment in her face. Disappointment that he had a child? Or that he was proving her jaundiced views of locums correct? 'I'll make sure the hospital isn't billed for the time I've had to take off.'

'Fine.'

'And thanks for looking after Ryan.'

She shrugged. 'No problem.'

Clearly it was, but there was nothing he could do about it right now.

He collected Eliot, walked him to the car and then sat on the bonnet out of Eliot's earshot while he rang Fran.

'Hello?'

'Fran, it's Eliot.'

'Oh.' She sounded flustered, then suddenly snapped into the sullen mode he'd grown used to over the last couple of months. Ever since she'd been seeing this Jon person. 'Are you going to be late again?'

'No. Early, in fact. I wondered if you had anything missing?'

'No.'

His mouth tightened. It must have taken Ryan half an hour to get here. And she still had no idea he was missing? 'Check your handbag,' he advised coldly.

'What?' She sounded slightly scared. 'Why?'

'Just check your handbag, then come back to the phone.'

Thirty seconds later, she was shrieking. 'My purse has gone!'

'It's here. With Ryan.'

'Ryan? I, um… No, he's in his room, making models.'

'He's sitting in my car, in the hospital car park,' Eliot corrected her. 'I think we've got some talking to do—don't you?'

'Eliot, I'm sorry, it's just—'

'Save it.' She hadn't even asked if the boy was all right. Hell, hell, hell. How had he managed to get it so wrong when he'd hired Fran? At the time she'd seemed young but sensible and Ryan hadn't minded her. Maybe he'd just been so desperate to find someone that he'd seen what he'd been looking for rather than what had really been there. 'Ryan's already explained. We're on our way home now.' If Fran had any sense, her boyfriend would be long gone before Eliot arrived. And he'd check the house over before she left. Get the locks changed tomorrow. And he'd need at least one day off... This was rapidly turning into a nightmare.

He consoled himself—just—with the thought that at least Ryan was OK. He'd found his way across Ludbury without any problems, he wasn't hurt. He'd sort this mess out, one step at a time.

And then he'd face Claire.

A personal problem. He could say that again. Claire wasn't sure whether she was angrier on Eliot's behalf or with Eliot himself. Angry because Ryan was much too young to have travelled across Ludbury by bus on his own—particularly a journey that involved changing buses. And angry because Eliot hadn't said a word about his personal circumstances. He'd let everyone assume that he was young, free and single.

To think that she'd nearly fallen for him...

Stick with your career, she told herself firmly. That at least won't let you down.

All the same, she was smarting again over that near clinch with Eliot, so she was relieved when Tilly called her over to look at one of their newer babies and she could concentrate on work again. 'Second-born twin, born at thirty-five weeks gestation,' Tilly said. 'The symptoms developed about an hour after birth so they've sent her up here in case it's RDS.' Respiratory distress syndrome was common in premature babies because their lungs hadn't matured enough yet. 'Her breathing's fast, she's grunting a bit, she's got nasal flaring and intercostal recession.'

Claire noted the way the baby's skin sucked in between and under her ribs. 'She's, what, two hours old now?'

'Yes.'

Claire listened to the baby's lungs. 'The air entry's reduced and I can hear creps.' She did some more checks. 'Heart rate 125 a minute, low blood pressure.' They could both see that the baby was lying in the 'frog' position, not moving as much as they'd expect from a new-born. 'OK. We need the usual bloods—hae-moglobin, white-blood count, platelets, gases, blood group and cross-match. Check the elec-trolytes, creatinine and calcium so we've got a baseline; blood culture plus deep ear and throat swabs to rule out any infection; and a chest X-ray to check we don't have any extra prob-lems.'

Gently, she stroked the baby's cheek. 'Hang on in there, little one. I know it's tiring, but we'll soon help you breathe more easily.' She looked at Tilly. 'Is the mum downstairs?'

Tilly nodded. 'Probably frantic—and pan-icking in case the other twin has the same problem.'

'I'll go down and see her,' Claire said. She rang down to the maternity unit, then went to see Carla Jennings.

'I'm Claire Thurman, senior registrar on the neonatal ward,' she said. 'I thought you'd like an update on Gillian.'

'Is she going to be all right?'

'We hope so. We're doing some tests at the moment, but I'm fairly sure she has what we call RDS—respiratory distress syndrome. It's fairly common in premature babies, and second-born twins are more likely than the first-born to get it. All it means is that she's having problems breathing because her lungs aren't mature enough. We're going to keep her warm, give her some oxygen to help her breathe and, depending on the test results, some synthetic surfactant to make her lungs mature.'

'Surfactant? Isn't that something to do with detergent?' Carla asked, frowning.

'Sort of—surfactant's a wetting agent which reduces surface tension. With detergents, the surfactant stops the water forming a skin. Pulmonary surfactant is secreted by the air sacs in your lungs and it basically stops your lungs collapsing when you breathe out. If a baby has RDS, his lungs haven't got enough surfactant so they don't inflate properly and he has trouble breathing,' Claire explained.

Carla nodded. 'Can I see her? Can I feed her?'

'See her, touch her, hold her, yes,' Claire said, 'but babies with RDS can't feed by mouth for a few days. We'll give her food through an intravenous line, so she'll get all the nutrition she needs.'

'I was going to breastfeed,' Carla said. 'I had it all planned. I'd practised with dolls at antenatal classes.'

'You still can,' Claire said, 'just not for the first couple of days. Though you can express milk for her if you'd like to. You can come and see her any time, and bring this little one with you. May I?'

'Oh—yes. Her name's Hayley.'

With a smile, Claire leaned over and picked up the baby, breathing in the distinctive, almost nutty smell of the newborn. 'She's beautiful. You must be very proud.'

'Oh, I am.' Tears glittered in her eyes, and Claire wasn't sure whether they were from joy at having Hayley or from fear about Gillian. Carla's next words confirmed it. 'But I'm so scared about little Gilly.'

'Of course you are. But you can see her whenever you like. It might look a bit scary, though,' Claire warned. 'As I said, we'll be feeding her by IV line and she'll have a head-box around her for two or three days so she gets warmed, humidified oxygen to help her breathe more easily. RDS does tend to get worse in the first twenty-four to thirty-six hours because the baby starts getting tired, but if we're lucky it'll be a mild case, and as soon as the surfactant starts to be produced when she's a day and a half old, she'll start to get better.'

'When will you know if it's this RDS?'

'As soon as the test results come back, in a couple of hours. I'll make sure someone comes in and tells you as soon as there's any news,' Claire promised. 'I just wanted to come and see you myself, so you weren't sitting down here worrying and not knowing what was going on.'

'Thank you,' Carla said. 'Can I come and see her now?'

'If the midwives think you're up to it. I'll have a word on my way out,' Claire said. 'And if you're worried at any time, just ask them to ring me.'

'I will.'

Claire had a quick word with the midwives at the nurses' station, then headed back up to the neonatal ward. 'The mum's coming up as soon as they give the go-ahead downstairs,' she told Tilly. 'So it's the usual for Gillian—continuous ECG, arterial catheters so we can measure blood gases, continuous monitoring of blood pressure and respiratory activity.'

'Plus temperature and pulse every three hours,' Tilly added. 'Do you want an IV line or umbilical artery catheter for the glucose-electrolyte infusion?'

'UAC,' Claire said. 'And before you ask, Tills—yes, I'll do it. Why do my staff all hate needles?'

CHAPTER FOUR

'Morning,' Eliot said, smiling at Claire.

'Morning.' No smile, and her voice was very cool.

Oh, hell. This was going to be even worse than he'd feared. She didn't really like children—apart from her patients—and she clearly wasn't happy that he'd left early two days previously and had had to take yesterday off, too. He'd let her down. But what else could he have done in the circumstances? 'Um—this is for you.'

'For me?'

She opened the envelope. It contained a card bearing a picture of a dinosaur, labelled *Iguanadon*. Inside, in the same spiky, childish handwriting was the message, *Thank you for looking after me. From Ryan. XO.*

'He told me to tell you that the O means a hug,' Eliot added.

'Tell him thanks for me. It's beautifully drawn.'

Still frosty. But was it his imagination or was there a tiny crack in her armour? He decided to take the gamble. After all, he had nothing left to lose. 'Can I have a private word, please?'

'I have a round to do.'

He couldn't let this go. He just couldn't. Claire was the first person he could ever remember Ryan talking about—so his son had recognised how special she was, too. 'Please. I promise I won't keep you more than five minutes.'

There was a long silence and for a moment he thought he'd pushed her too far. Then she nodded. 'All right. Five minutes.'

He followed her to her office in silence and closed the door behind them. 'Firstly, I'd like to thank you for looking after Ryan.'

'You already have.' She shrugged. 'And there's no need.'

'I think there is. You're the first person in a very long time who's treated Ryan as a normal child.'

'Because he has Asperger's, you mean?'

Eliot held her gaze without flinching at the words. 'Yes. Most people just sense there's something different about him and back off.

He told me about the milk—how you poured it with the wrong hand but it was OK because you told him why and you let him tell you when to stop.'

'I make the same sort of bargains with Jed.'

'Jed?'

'My godson. He has Asperger's, too.' Asperger's was a type of autism which had a classic 'triad' of difficulties—communication, social skills and rigidity of thought. Children with the syndrome—most commonly boys— often had a high IQ but were loners, found group work difficult, found it easier to talk to adults rather than other children and took language very literally.

'And that's how you picked it up?' he guessed. 'Because he's like Jed?'

She shrugged. 'And it's my job. I'm a paediatrician.'

'Neonatal specialist,' he corrected. 'Asperger's isn't like classic autism—there are no obvious learning difficulties and it's often not diagnosed until a child starts school.'

'No.'

'But he liked you.'

Eliot's little boy liked her. Claire's stomach clenched. That was as much as she'd get from any child, liking. Possibly a niece or nephew might feel a deep affection for her, but not the same love a child felt for a parent. Not that same deep, unbreakable bond.

She forced the thought away. She'd come to terms with not being able to have children years ago. She wasn't going to let that change now. 'Was there something else?' she asked coolly, praying that Eliot would just let it go.

'Yes. I wanted to explain about the other day. Ryan came here because his childminder had been…' He paused, with a grimace. 'Entertaining her boyfriend. So Ryan got sick of being on his own and decided to find his own way here. I sacked Fran and she's not going to get a good reference—but, I'm sorry, I'll need to take more time off over the next few days to sort out a new childminder.' He sighed. 'One who can actually cope with Ryan. It's not all Fran's fault. I should have made sure she was comfortable working with a child who has special needs.'

Claire couldn't help asking. 'What about your wife? Can't she take time off as well?'

Eliot gave a mirthless laugh. 'My ex-wife hasn't seen Ryan for five years.'

Claire stared at him in shock. 'Five *years*?' He'd been coping on his own for that long?

A muscle flickered in his jaw. 'I'm sorry, I shouldn't be burdening you with my problems. I'll try not to let things get in the way of my work.'

Claire flinched. She knew she deserved that. 'If you'd said something before, I might have been able to help.'

He raked a hand through his hair. 'Yeah. Maybe. I suppose I'm just a bit…well, sensitive where Ryan's concerned. I don't want anything to hurt him.' He closed his eyes. 'Bit late, where Fran's concerned. Obviously my judgement in childminders is completely off.'

Claire thought fast. 'There's a crèche for hospital staff—there's a huge waiting list but I think I can pull some strings, at least for a couple of days. If you can get Ryan here by taxi after school, you'll be able to pick him up after work.'

'How do you mean, pull strings for me?' he queried, opening his eyes to stare at her.

Claire shrugged. 'Jed's mother Ally is my best friend. And she just happens to run the hospital crèche. She might be able to fit Ryan into the after-school club for a couple of afternoons. I can't promise anything long term but at least it'll buy you some time. And Ally's bound to know some childminders who are used to working with children with special needs.'

Hope flickered in his eyes. 'Could you put her in touch with me?'

'Sure.'

'You're a lifesaver.' Impulsively, he hugged her.

Mistake, Claire thought, her senses on red alert. Back away now. Pull rank. Do anything, but get out of his arms. Because if you stay here for one more second you'll do something stupid. Like hold him.

Too late. Her arms were already round him. She could smell the scent of his shower gel, clean and citrusy. She could feel his heartbeat—a little unsteady, a little fast. Just like her own.

His lips brushed her cheek. Gently. Sweetly.

Pull away, she told herself urgently.

But she didn't. She simply moved her head so that her mouth was next to his. Time seemed to slow, and then his lips were brushing against hers. Lightly, at first, questioning, and then as she responded he drew her closer, deepening the kiss.

It felt as if fireworks were going off inside her head. Starbursts, rockets, whistling.

Whistling?

She pulled back. Thank God, her door was still closed and because she hadn't opened the blinds yet this morning, no one in the ward could have seen what had just happened. Or wolf-whistled at seeing a clinch like that in the middle of the ward.

She only hoped that her lips weren't red and swollen. They were certainly tingling. And Eliot looked as dazed as she felt. Oh, no. No, no, no. This couldn't happen. Particularly when she was just about to go on a ward round. She was Claire Thurman, professional neonatalogist—she never, but never did this sort of thing. Absolutely not, since Paddy.

'I've got a ward round to do.'

Her voice definitely didn't sound like her own. She sounded as if a steamroller had just run over her. Hell, she *felt* as if a steamroller had just run over her! A feeling she hadn't had since the first time Paddy had kissed her. And even that faded into insignificance compared with what had just happened.

'Claire. I...um...look, I didn't mean to do that.'

'Neither did I.' The words were out before she could stop them. She lifted her chin. 'We're colleagues.'

'Professionals,' Eliot said. Though his eyes were saying something different. Something that made her blood tingle and her pulse quicken. Something that made her whole body react. Something that made her want to step back into his arms and let him kiss her again. Let him hold her, touch her, caress her to paradise and back.

'Professionals,' she echoed.

So why couldn't she move? Why couldn't she just pick up her paperwork and do her ward round? Why was she still staring at him, unable to tear her gaze away from his?

'Lunch. How about lunch?' he asked.

'There's no need.'

'Please. Let me.'

Lunch? Or was he asking something else? No. Oh, no. That kiss had definitely wiped out a few brain cells. She shook her head, trying to clear it, but it didn't work. She was still in this weird parallel universe where her patients were waiting for her but all she could think about was Eliot's mouth. And where she wanted it to be.

'I owe you a proper explanation.'

'OK.' Her mouth wasn't connected to her common sense, that much was sure.

'Half twelve in the canteen.'

'Half twelve in the canteen,' she echoed.

How she got through her ward round and paperwork that morning, she had no idea. But at half past twelve she was sitting at a quiet table in the corner of the staff canteen opposite Eliot.

'This ought to be—I dunno. Somewhere posh. Something special.'

'A chicken sandwich here is fine.' Not that she was going to be able to eat it. A thousand butterflies were rampaging round her stomach and there wasn't any room for anything else.

She looked at him. Saw the fine lines of strain etched at the corners of his eyes. Saw the shadows underneath them. He'd clearly been worried for a long, long time. A single parent who had no one to share his fears with, no one to reassure him that he was doing his best and he'd made all the right decisions.

At least he is a parent—you'll never be one.

She pushed the thought away. Her problems couldn't be sorted. Eliot's, on the other hand, could. 'Tell me what happened,' she invited softly.

'You don't want to know.'

He sounded tired. Bone-deep tired. She wanted to hold him, tell him it was OK. Let him lose himself in her…

Whoa, there, she told herself. Take it slowly. One step at a time. Just because he kissed you, it doesn't mean he wants anything more. And you can't afford any wishful thinking. 'I wouldn't be asking if I didn't want to know.'

Eliot looked at her. Was this his boss talking, with the aim of solving her staffing problems? But, no, there was something in her face. Compassion. Kindness. *Interest.*

So he started talking. Saying the words he'd kept to himself for so very, very long. And once he started, he found he couldn't stop.

'I met Malandra when we were students. She wasn't a medic—she was reading economics—and somehow we just clicked. We moved in together when she'd graduated. I still had two more years of being a student and a year as a houseman, but it didn't matter. She got a job with a financial services company and she studied for her exams when I was on call or working late at the hospital. Everything was just as we'd planned.' His mouth twisted. 'And then one day she told me she was pregnant. It was completely unexpected—we'd never even talked about having children.

'She thought about having a termination, then she had a miscarriage scare and realised she wanted the baby, even though I was still a student. We thought we'd manage financially and being parents would be easy. So we got married.' He raked a hand through his hair. 'We didn't have a clue, and Ryan was a difficult baby. He never slept, and he hated being cuddled or having a fuss made of him. And because I was in my first job as a houseman—you know what kind of hours junior doctors work—I wasn't there enough. I left Malandra to cope too much on her own.'

'Hey, you can't dictate when you're on call—especially in your first post. It's not your fault.'

'It feels like it. I was a qualified doctor, and I had no idea my own wife had postnatal depression and my son had an autistic spectrum disorder. I had no idea how scared Malandra was about Ryan, that she thought she was a useless mother and he didn't love her because he hated being cuddled and he never looked at her, and it was all her fault.'

'If she didn't tell you about it—' Claire began.

'But I never asked,' Eliot cut in. 'I just *assumed* she was coping. Sure, I realised that Ryan wasn't like any of the other babies we knew, but I thought it was just a boy thing—everyone else at our antenatal group had quiet little girls. Apart from my patients at the hospital, I'd never had that much to do with babies. Neither of us had. Malandra and I were both only children.'

'A lot of new parents haven't had much to do with babies before their own arrives,' Claire said gently. 'Don't be too hard on yourself.'

'But I was a med student. I'd studied this—I should have known there was something wrong because his eye contact was poor—even now, Ryan will watch your mouth rather than your whole face and you have to keep reminding him. And then the tantrums started... Terrible tantrums. Ryan would throw himself on the floor, bang his head, scream—all because the dustbin lorry hadn't gone as far round the corner as it usually did, or because Malandra hadn't let him walk through the gate first, or she'd used the wrong bowl for his breakfast. Any change to his routine and he went bananas.'

'Why didn't Malandra talk to her health visitor about it? Say, at the eighteen-month check?'

'Because she thought she was supposed to cope. She thought she was the problem, not Ryan—he never seemed too bad when I was around, and I suppose I thought part of it was because Malandra was sick of being trapped at home with a baby when she'd had all these plans for a glamorous career. We seemed to be muddling through.' Eliot crumbled the corners of his sandwich. 'And then one day I came home and Ryan was in his cot, crying. On his own. His nappy was soaking, and so were his clothes. Malandra wasn't there. I was frantic— I couldn't believe she'd left him on his own. He was two years old, that's all. Just *two*. And if he'd climbed out of that cot...' His face tightened with anguish, with the remembered fear of what could have happened.

Claire took his hand and squeezed it. 'But he didn't.'

'Yeah. Anyway, I cleaned him up and calmed him down. The place was a mess—papers piled everywhere, and so many toys on the floor that you couldn't even see the carpet. I started clearing up and then I found the note. Malandra said she'd had enough and just couldn't cope any more. She was sorry, but she had to go.' He shrugged. 'I tracked her down in the end through her parents and some friends. She wouldn't talk to me, but at least I knew she was safe. And I took some leave so I could look after Ryan.'

'On your own?'

He nodded. 'Her parents didn't want to know, and mine—well, my dad was very ill and my mum really didn't need the extra worry, so I didn't tell them. To be honest, I thought Malandra would just stay away for a few days, long enough to think things through and give me a bit of a scare. I always thought she'd come back to us and we'd sort things out. It took a month before I realised she wasn't ever coming home. So I put Ryan on the waiting list with a few crèches and child-minders, and took a career break so I could look after him.'

'And that's when you realised he wasn't like other children?'

Eliot nodded. 'I noticed the routine thing, and the way he used to line his toys up. If you moved a single one out of line, it'd take him half an hour to calm down again. Just sobbing, incoherent rage. I got help in the end, but it took a long time to get him diagnosed. At first everyone seemed to think I was just a paranoid parent who'd read a lot and knew too much and was—well, you know what it's like when you're a med student. You read the textbooks and start seeing the symptoms in yourself. Except they thought I was seeing the symptoms in Ryan, not me.'

'Ally went through something similar when she was trying to get a diagnosis for Jed,' Claire said. 'But you've coped on your own for five years *and* you're still working as a doctor. That's one hell of an achievement.'

'Most days it doesn't feel like it,' Eliot said.

'Most days you just wish your little boy was like every other little boy. Getting into scrapes but getting out of them again, having friends over for tea after school, driving you bananas with requests for the latest toy if he's a very, very, very good boy, and then melting you by telling you he loves you and you're the best dad in the world—no, the universe.'

Eliot was stunned. Could she read his mind? 'How do you know all that?' The question was out before he could stop it.

'That's how Ally feels. And she's married to the most supportive man in the world,' Claire said quietly. 'You're having to do it all on your own, so it's not surprising you're finding it tough.'

Eliot lifted his chin. He definitely didn't want her pity. Not when he could still remember how it felt to kiss her, how it felt when she responded to him. 'I'll manage.'

The words that had half formed in Claire's head decided to bypass her common sense and go straight out of her mouth. 'But you don't have to. I'll help.'

'I'm not looking for a replacement wife,' Eliot said tightly.

Oh, hell—me and my big mouth, Claire thought. He thinks I'm moving in on him after that kiss this morning... She took a deep breath. 'I'm not offering to be a replacement wife. Or anything else. I'm not making a pass at you, Eliot.' *Liar.* You know you want to, a little voice taunted in her head. After that kiss, you want more. 'I don't want a relationship. I'm concentrating on my career.' It was her stock answer since she'd finally stopped believing in Paddy. It had convinced everyone else, so it should convince Eliot—shouldn't it?

'So what are you saying?' he asked.

'It looks as if you and Ryan could use a friend. I understand what you're going through because someone very close to me has been through something similar. So I'm offering friendship.'

There was a long, long pause. A pause that made the back of her neck grow hot and the ends of her fingers tingle. Was his pride going to make him push her away?

And then at last he looked at her. 'Yeah, you're right. We could use a friend. Thank you.'

So that made it official. They were friends. Nothing less...but nothing more.

CHAPTER FIVE

'CLAIRE, can you come down to Theatre?' Shannon asked. 'I've got a mum with pea soup. Forty-two weeks.'

Claire recognised the shorthand—the mum was overdue and her waters had broken to reveal thick green meconium, a bowel movement the baby had passed in the uterus. If the baby swallowed it during the birth—known as meconium aspiration syndrome, or MAS—it could cause a lot of problems.

'I'm on my way,' Claire said.

Around fifteen to twenty per cent of babies born later than forty-one weeks gestation passed meconium in the uterus. Most of the time there were just thin traces of green in the waters and there was no problem, but if the baby had passed a lot of meconium, the waters would be thicker and there was a much greater risk of the baby breathing in some meconium and needing special care.

'Hi, I'm Claire Thurman, the paediatrician,' Claire said to the panting woman in the delivery suite.

'Is something wrong with my baby?' she asked, her eyes panic-stricken.

'No, I'm just here to do a routine check when your little one makes an appearance,' Claire reassured her. 'Not long now.'

At delivery, the baby's skin, nails and umbilical cord were stained with meconium: a bad sign. Claire quickly cleared the baby's upper airways and used a laryngoscope to check for more signs of meconium. To her dismay, she saw traces of meconium at the baby's vocal cords. She had no choice: she had to intubate and do tracheal suction. Listening to the chest revealed added sounds and crepitation, and she noticed bowing of the sternum: the classic signs of air trapping. Once she was sure that the baby was stable, she came to sit by the parents and held both their hands.

'We need to take your little girl up to Special Care so we can keep an eye on her and make sure she doesn't get any infections. I know this must be very worrying for you,' she said softly, 'but I can promise you she'll be in the best hands and you can see her whenever you like.'

'Leila. Her name's Leila,' Barbara Chatwyn said, her voice shaking.

'It's a lovely name,' Claire said. 'What happened is that, in common with a lot of late babies, she passed a bowel movement while she was inside you. She breathed some of it in while she was being born, and it can cause a bit of air to be trapped in her lungs so her lungs inflate too much. That means there's a risk she might develop a pneumothorax—that's where air gets trapped between the membranes that cover the lungs. There's also a risk that the meconium can give her a bacterial infection, so what we want to do is give her some antibiotics to make sure she doesn't get an infection. We're also going to keep an eye on her breathing, blood pressure and fluids to make sure her lungs are working properly.'

'She's going to be all right?' Paul Chatwyn asked.

'She should be fine, though she'll need to spend a week or so with us,' Claire said. 'I'm going to get a cot sorted out for her upstairs, and then I'll be back to oversee her transfer. Then I'll introduce you to my colleague, Dr

Eliot Slater. He and one of my senior nurses will be looking after her while I'm on leave for the rest of the week. Now, I think young Leila wants a cuddle with her mum,' she said with a smile. 'I'll see you very soon.'

Once back on the ward, she found Eliot. 'I've got an MAS case coming upstairs in a couple of minutes,' she said. 'I'd like you to look after her.'

'Sure. Broad-spectrum antibiotic prophylaxis and keep a chest-drain kit to hand?' he asked.

She loved the way his mind kept pace with hers. He really was perfect to work with. 'Please.'

'It'll all be in hand and you can just enjoy your days off.' He bit his lip. 'Well, not that it *is* time off.'

'Oh, yes, it is,' Claire assured him. 'Your son and I have plans. We're meeting up with Ally and Jed for a pirate picnic at Ludlow castle, and we're going to the astronomy centre—things you can't do on your own.'

She made it sound as if he was doing her a favour, not the other way round. It was one hell of an imposition: half-term week, when the childminder she'd helped him find wasn't able to look after Ryan for the whole week, and Claire had announced that she had way too much leave stored up and she'd rather use it than lose it, so she was taking the second half of the week off and spending it with Ryan.

How could Eliot help but feel guilty? Especially as she was the one who'd declared she didn't want children. And here she was, using her precious leave on *his* son. 'Are you sure?'

'I wouldn't have offered if I hadn't meant it,' Claire said. She punched him lightly on the arm. 'You worry too much.'

'Yeah.' Though his worries had been halved for the last month. Claire had introduced him to Ally, who'd helped find him a new child-minder, a woman Ryan clearly adored because he actually talked to his father about Mrs Forrest and how nice she was. Claire had taken Ryan to school when she'd been on a late and Eliot on an early, and she'd taken Ryan to tea with Ally and Jed. For the first time Eliot could remember, Ryan had a proper friend of his own, a child who shared his love of dinosaurs and maps and undersea creatures.

The only sticking point was that he and Claire had agreed on friendship. And he was having the most vivid X-rated dreams about her. But she'd made it clear that her terms were friendship and nothing more, and if that was the only way he could have her in his life, he'd have to put up with it.

He dragged his mind back to work. 'I'll get the cot sorted out. Do you want me to oversee the transfer?'

She shook her head. 'That's OK. The parents are expecting me. I'll introduce you to them when I bring them here. See you in a bit.'

The perfect team at work. The perfect team outside—Ryan was so like Jed that Claire had felt no awkwardness with him, and he and Eliot had slipped so easily into her life. The only sticking point was the agreement she and Eliot had made about friendship. But she knew she couldn't offer him anything else—there was no point in starting a relationship when she wasn't able to take it through to its logical conclusion, marriage and a brother or sister for Ryan.

Friendship was enough. It had to be. And when she wasn't with him she'd concentrate on getting her promotion—work would stop her thinking of Eliot and dreaming of what might have been. Remembering that kiss. Or wondering what it would be like if...

No. It wasn't going to happen. And that was that.

'Hi, I'm home,' Eliot called, closing the front door behind him.

Home. Since Claire had been in their lives, it really did feel like home, not just the place where he lived. Knowing that she was going to be there tonight when he got back after his shift had sent a warm glow through him all the way home.

'Daddy!' A small figure rushed towards him at speed. 'Guess what, we're making cakes! I helped Claire and—'

'Whoa there, tiger.' Eliot scooped his son into his arms, smiling. The last month had made such a difference to their lives. Since Claire had been around, Ryan had blossomed. He even ran to Eliot with his arms wide for a hug, instead of wriggling away as soon as he could. It was like being a proper family.

Except he couldn't impose that much on Claire.

Ryan was still chattering about making cakes and explaining the chemical reaction of eggs, air and flour when combined with heat when Eliot carried him into the kitchen. Eliot grinned when he saw the smear of flour across Claire's nose. 'I wish I had a film in the camera. Then, next time you were being bossy on the ward, I'd have some ammunition.'

'Ha, ha.' Claire grinned back and pulled a face at him. 'So how's Leila doing?'

'You're supposed to be off duty,' he reminded her.

'I was—for the last three days. I'm back on tomorrow, so I want to know what's happening on the ward.' Claire shrugged. 'OK. I'll ring Tilly later and ask her, then.'

Eliot rolled his eyes. 'You're impossible.'

'Meconium aspiration syndrome isn't very common. And I don't want Leila ending up with—'

'A pneumothorax,' Eliot finished. 'Relax. She's fine. And, yes, we're checking for fluid overload, checking her blood pressure, doing regular blood gases—'

'And I should just shut up and stop nagging,' Claire said with a rueful look.

He smiled. 'You said it. Claire, you know we'd page you if we were worried. There's nothing to report. She's doing well.'

'Good.'

'It was raining today so we couldn't go to the park. That's why we made cakes. Did you know, we drink the same water that the Romans did, hundreds of days ago?' Ryan asked, wriggling down from Eliot's arms.

'We did the water cycle today,' Claire mouthed to Eliot above Ryan's head.

The day before yesterday had been telescopes, following their trip to the astronomy centre. Yesterday had been pirates after the picnic at Ludlow castle—a picnic where apparently Ally and Claire had dressed as pirates as well. Eliot had had a bad moment, imagining Claire in tight black trousers, a filmy white blouse, a pirate's hat and a crimson velvet waistcoat.

And now the water cycle. Hell. His imagination went straight into overdrive, imagining Claire as a mermaid swimming in a clear pool with her hair loose and streaming behind her. And he temporarily lost his common sense— that was the only explanation he could think of as to why he leaned forward and brushed the smear of flour from her nose. And then leaned closer and licked her top lip.

She stared at him in what looked like disbelief.

'Crumb,' he muttered. An imaginary one.

'Right.' Her tone said she didn't believe him, and he didn't dare look at her. But how could he possibly explain that he'd imagined her as a mermaid and had barely stopped himself kissing her?

He took refuge in a safe topic. 'So, what cakes have you made, Ryan?'

'Lemon drizzle cake. You have to mix the lemon juice with the sugar so it melts, then pour it over the cake so it soaks in and makes it lemony. If you don't have the sugar it goes straight to the bottom and the cake goes soggy.'

'He'll be a top chef before you know it,' Claire said.

You really, really have to get a grip on yourself, Eliot thought. Stop thinking about whipped cream, melted chocolate and what you'd like to do with them. Claire's off limits. A friend. Nothing more. Understand?

His mind agreed. His heart and certain other parts of his anatomy didn't.

'Want to try some?'

Down, boy, Eliot admonished himself. She's talking about *cake*. 'I'd love to.'

How he got through the rest of the evening, he never knew. Spaghetti and garlic bread cooked by Claire with 'help' from Ryan, followed by ice cream and a sauce made from melted Mars bars, and then rich, dark coffee made by Claire while he read Ryan a bedtime story.

It would be so, so easy to take the coffeecup from her hand, put it on the table and then kiss her. Kiss her the way he'd kissed her that morning in her office. Kiss her until both of them were reeling.

But common sense prevailed. Just. And then she handed him a letter. 'What's this?'

'It arrived this morning. Have a look.'

His eyes widened when he read it. 'Miss Thurman, neonatal consultant? I take it you're going to accept the post?'

'Uh-huh.'

'Hey. That's great. You deserve it. I'm really pleased for you.' Even though it put her even further out of his reach. What could he offer her? He was a locum who'd never make it up the career scale, a single parent whose child had special needs and the most claims on his time. And she'd just been made consultant at a very young age. She had a glittering future and he couldn't hold her back.

'So I thought we'd go out and celebrate tomorrow night.'

She was asking him out? No. Them. She was asking *them* out.

'Is Ryan OK with lights?'

'Lights?' What did lights have to do with it?

'I thought we could go and see that new 3-D movie—but I know some children with autistic spectrum disorders react badly to flickering lights.'

'No, he's fine.'

'Good. Jed loved it. I thought maybe the pictures followed by a meal out?'

'As long as you let me pay.'

'My celebration, my bill.'

'Your celebration, my treat,' Eliot corrected. 'I'll book the tickets. What time do you want me to pick you up?'

'Pick me up?'

'We may as well go in the same car.'

'OK. Seven?'

'Sounds good.' She retrieved her letter. 'I'd better go. I'm on an early tomorrow.'

'Yeah. Claire?'

'Mmm-hmm?'

'I just wanted to say thanks for all you've done with Ryan.'

'Pleasure. See you tomorrow night.'

It wasn't a date. It was a celebration—at her suggestion—as friends. Ryan was coming with them. So why was she taking so much care with her make-up and her hair? And why had she treated herself to a new bottle of perfume?

'You're being a fool. He isn't interested. He sees you as a friend and he's grateful that you're helping him sort out his life, but he thinks of you more as his big sister. He's even told you that,' she informed her reflection. 'Jeans and a T-shirt would have done.' But she hadn't been able to resist wearing what Ryan called her pirate trousers, smart black velvet teamed with a lacy vest top. And she couldn't help the butterflies in her stomach either, while she was waiting for Eliot. It *felt* like a proper date, even though it was officially a date for three.

And then the doorbell went.

She deliberately took her time answering it.

'Hi, there.'

'For you.'

She gaped at the bouquet of perfect long-stemmed white roses. 'They're beautiful. Thank you. But…'

'Mixture of thanks for this week and congrats on making it as a consultant,' Eliot told her.

'And these are from me,' Ryan added, handing her a gold box. 'Thank you for having me this week. I chose them. I showed the man in the shop which ones to put in.'

She grinned, imagining just how precise Ryan had been about which chocolate he'd picked from each flavour. 'And you can help me share them later. They're lovely. Thank you, sweetheart. I'll put my beautiful flowers in water and I'll be right with you.'

Roses. Eliot had bought her roses. But not red ones, the traditional declaration of love. These were a formal thank you. Nothing more.

'I knew she was going to wear her pirate trousers,' Ryan whispered.

'They're cool,' Eliot whispered back. Though that didn't nearly cover his feelings. Claire looked stunning. When she'd opened the door, he'd had to shove the roses at her to stop himself blurting out something stupid. Like, 'You look gorgeous and I want to go to bed with you right now.' He'd almost wished he was dropping Ryan off at his grandparents' house and was going out with Claire on his own. To a quiet, exclusive restaurant which served perfect food. Followed by a walk on the beach in the moonlight. Followed by—

No. Apart from the fact that Ryan no longer had grandparents—his parents were both dead and Malandra's parents had refused to have anything to do with Eliot or Ryan since she'd walked out—it couldn't have happened anyway. He and Claire were just friends.

Eliot had himself back under control by the time Claire rejoined them. He drove them into the middle of Ludbury and picked up their pre-booked cinema tickets and card-and-Cellophane glasses.

'What are these for?' Ryan asked.

'It's so you can see the three-D effect—it makes it look as if things are coming right out of the screen. Including the dinosaurs,' Claire explained. 'There are pink and green lines around the dinosaurs on the film, so if you see it without glasses it looks a bit odd. If you put the glasses on, the coloured Cellophane cancels out the lines and makes the background look further back.'

'But you can take them off at any time if your eyes hurt,' Eliot added. 'And if it's too loud for you, just say and we'll go.'

'You've never taken him to the pictures?' Claire mouthed over Ryan's head.

'No,' Eliot mouthed back, feeling guilty and anxious that maybe Ryan wouldn't be able to cope with it.

It must have been written all over his face because she gave him a reassuring wink. 'Trust me, he'll *love* this,' she mouthed. 'Right—are we having toffee or salty popcorn, Ryan?'

'Toffee, please!' the little boy responded.

Eliot found he couldn't really concentrate on the film, despite the fast pace and lots of action. He couldn't stop himself thinking about what it would be like, going to the pictures with Claire. Right now they were in one of the middle rows, with Ryan between them. But in his fantasy they were sitting in the back row. He was sliding him arm round her, breathing in her perfume—a rich, sweet vanilla scent with a hint of something else he couldn't quite place but liked a lot. He was feeding her popcorn, feeling her lips against his fingers. And then he'd kiss her. Slowly. Tiny kisses. Teasing her mouth open. She'd kiss him back and they'd forget the film, lost in each other, and...

Oh hell. It's just as well we're in the dark and she can't see the effect my imagination's just had on me, he thought wryly.

Claire, on the other side of Ryan, glanced across at Eliot. He had one arm thrown around his son's shoulders. It was so easy to imagine herself in the seat next to him, with his arm around *her* shoulder. She could almost smell the clean citrus scent of his aftershave. And then they'd repeat the kiss they'd shared in her office—only this time it would be even better. Maybe they'd prolong the torment by going out for dinner after the pictures, and his foot would slide against hers under the table, promising future delights. Or maybe they just wouldn't be able to wait. They'd go back to her place and make love...

She dragged her thoughts away with an effort. Hell. They were supposed to be friends. They'd even agreed it. He wasn't in the market for a relationship—Ryan had to come first. And she couldn't offer him anything more than friendship anyway. She just had to remember that.

CHAPTER SIX

THE following Saturday, when both Claire and Eliot were off duty, they arranged to take Ryan to London to see the dinosaurs. Neither of them told Ryan where they were going, just that it was a surprise and he'd love it.

They caught the train at Birmingham and Ryan read their destination on the ticket reservation. 'We're going to London?' he asked, eyes round with wonder.

'Yes. We're going to see some special things,' Eliot said.

'What sort of things?' Ryan wanted to know.

'How about dinosaurs?' Claire suggested.

'*Real* dinosaurs?'

'Real skeletons. And moving models.'

Ryan beamed. 'That's brilliant. That's really brilliant.'

When Eliot persuaded the ticket inspector to let the little boy stamp all their tickets on the way to London, Ryan was in ecstasy. 'Where are we going when we get to London?'

'To South Kensington first, to see the dinosaurs at the Natural History Museum,' Claire told him.

'Then we'll take a boat down to the Tower of London,' Eliot said, 'if it's not raining.'

Ryan looked up at the grey skies. 'It's not going to rain,' he said with a small child's confidence.

'And then we'll catch the tube at Tower Hill to Holborn, and see the mummies at the British Museum,' Claire told him. She gave him a map of the tube. 'We're going around London on the underground train system. See, each different train line here is a different colour.'

'The Circle line's yellow, the District's green, the Picca...' He stumbled over the word.

'Piccadilly line,' Eliot prompted.

'It's purple. And this red one's the Central line because it goes right through the centre.' Ryan pored over the little map, reading the station names to himself. Eliot grinned, knowing exactly what his son was doing. His favourite occupation: memorising map routes.

Ryan's excitement grew as they went onto the tube. 'Daddy's going to put his ticket in that slot there to make the gate open. He'll go first. Then I'll put your ticket in and you go when I say, "Go." Then I'll follow you,' Claire explained. Even so, Ryan made a dash for it too soon and was horrified when the gates closed in front of him. Then he hesitated after Claire had fed his ticket into the barrier and she had to yell, 'Go!' for a second time.

'We have to stand on the right on the escalators,' she said. 'Then people who are in a hurry can go down faster on the left.'

'It's a long way down,' Ryan said, peering into the long tunnel. 'You know, this is where they used to live in the war, when the bombs went off. And there are huge rats down here, as big as cats.'

'Your little boy knows a lot for his age, doesn't he?' a woman behind Claire said. 'It's nice to see a little 'un so interested.'

'Yes,' Claire said, smiling politely, though inside she could feel her heart ripping. *Her little boy.* How could anyone possibly make that mistake? Ryan didn't even look anything like her! Of course he wasn't her little boy. She never would have a little boy of her own. And spending a day like this with Eliot and Ryan, as if they were a proper family... Just who was she trying to kid?

They could never be a family. Friendship would just have to be enough.

She closed her eyes in pain. *Her little boy.* However many times she declared that she didn't want children, she still couldn't make herself believe it. Her biological clock had already started ticking, and since she'd met Eliot, the tick had been getting steadily louder. And even though her head knew it was pointless, that she *couldn't* have children, she still couldn't muffle that damned clock.

As for stopping things right now, before she got hurt…it was already way too late for that. Because she'd fallen in love with Eliot and his little boy. The family she couldn't have.

Eliot noticed that Claire was quiet, even a little distant, as they went onto the platform. Maybe it was just the underground system, he thought. It wasn't easy to have a conversation in the middle of a crowded platform or carriage. On the other hand, he was sure he could see pain in her eyes. But he had no idea what had hurt her, and he had a feeling that if he asked what was wrong she'd brush his concern aside and clam up even more.

If a genie had come along at that moment and offered him three wishes, he knew exactly what his first wish would be. To be able to read Claire's mind. But magic lamps only appeared in pantomimes. He'd just have to muddle through as best he could.

'You OK?' he asked casually.

'Yeah. I'm a bit like Ryan—I don't like crowds. No way could I handle the tube in the rush hour. If I worked in London, I'd have to live within walking distance of the hospital.'

She'd consider working in London? Well, of course she would. She was a neonatal specialist, and a good one. She'd be an asset to any children's hospital—any teaching hospital. And hadn't she made it clear that she was married to her career? It was obvious that she'd go to London or one of the big specialist centres one day.

He pushed the thought away. Concentrate on the here and now, he told himself. She's with you now. That's as much as you can ask for.

To his relief, Ryan coped well with the crowds, not shying away from the squash of people in the carriages. And when they went into the huge red building on Exhibition Road, both Claire and Eliot turned to watch Ryan's face as he saw his first dinosaur. 'It's huge!' he said, grinning widely. 'It's really *huge!*'

Ryan chattered happily all the way through the Life galleries and tugged at Claire's hand from time to time to point something out to her or ask a question. Eliot watched them. It felt as if they were a real family and his whole body throbbed with longing. *This* was what he wanted. His son, a job he loved, the woman of his dreams...

Hell. He really had it bad. This, he realised with shock, was love. He *loved* Claire. But she'd only offered him friendship. Nothing more. He had to remember that. Back off, he reminded himself sharply. Back off before you lose her even as a friend.

They stopped for a drink, visited the Earth galleries so Ryan could tell them everything he knew about meteorites and volcanoes, and then Ryan spotted a sign for the insect exhibition. 'Arachnids. They're spiders,' he said. 'Let's go and see if there's a big one!'

There wasn't, but he was delighted by the insect exhibition anyway—particularly the tank of ants. Claire shuddered and turned away from them. 'I don't mind spiders, but ants and daddy-long-legs—no way!'

'You're scared of ants?' Eliot asked in disbelief. 'But they're *tiny*!'

'Ever been bitten by a flying ant?' she asked.

'No.'

'If you had, you'd know why. I was ten when it happened. The bricks under our kitchen window were literally swarming with ants. Flying ones, too—and I got bitten several times. It felt as if someone had stabbed me with a red-hot needle. Since then, the first sign of an ant and I go into overdrive with the ant powder,' she told him.

'OK, I understand that. But what's the problem with crane flies?'

'At night,' she said. 'It's the way they bounce around lights. I can just imagine them getting in my hair and...' She shivered. 'Ugh.'

Eliot slid his arm around her shoulders and squeezed. 'Hey. Ring me next time you see a big scary daddy-long-legs, and I'll rescue you.'

'Huh.' She pulled a face at him but she didn't shrug his arm away. And Eliot couldn't have moved his arm from her shoulders if his life had depended on it. It wasn't part of their friendship agreement—it was very far from it, and light years away from what he'd promised himself he'd do—but it felt *right*, holding her close like that.

Ryan had memorised the tube map and directed them to Westminster so they could see Big Ben, and then they caught a boat to Tower Bridge. Somehow Eliot found himself holding Claire's hand on the boat. Rather than pulling away, she let his fingers slide between hers and even returned the slight pressure on his fingers. And when they wandered round the Tower of London, he was still holding her hand along the wall walks and in the queue to see the Crown Jewels and the armoury display.

'Henry the Eighth was really fat,' Ryan pronounced loudly. 'Look how big his armour is! He must have needed a really big horse to carry him. And he was a bad man. He chopped off his wife's head. He had lots of wives.'

Several people turned to look at the little boy, laughing. Eliot tensed.

'They're smiling *with* him,' Claire whispered in his ear, squeezing his fingers.

'Yeah. Sorry. I get over-protective,' he muttered.

'Of course you do. But he's fine. He's really enjoying himself.'

'Yeah.'

'Relax.'

Relax? Eliot thought. How can I, when I'm worried about Ryan and all I can think about is kissing you—and I know if I do that it'll push you away?

But he let her lead him out of the tower to the green outside where two men in Elizabethan dress were duelling.

'That's cool,' Ryan announced. 'I'm going to be a dueller when I grow up.'

He was equally taken by the ravens. 'I didn't think they'd be so, well, *black*,' he said. 'They're blacker than blackbirds.'

'They're bigger than I expected, too,' Eliot said.

'Dad, did you know if the ravens ever fly away from here, the kingdom will fall?' Ryan asked.

'Don't tell him their wings are clipped,' Eliot muttered into Claire's ear. 'Not unless you know exactly how it's done and whether it hurts and how old they are when it's done, and what the man's called who clips their wings…'

They posed for a picture with a Beefeater on their way out of the Tower of London, then let Ryan direct them to Holborn. This time, the little boy came unstuck on the escalators heading down to the platform.

'Stand on the right,' Eliot reminded him as Ryan stepped onto the left-hand side.

'Help!' Ryan said. He turned back and ran up the steps again.

Claire, who'd stepped on behind him, raced up after him and guided him to the queue on the right of the escalator. 'OK, honey, we're going to step on *this* side of the escalator. You go first,' she said gently, and followed him onto the steps.

Eliot was waiting for them at the bottom. 'By the time I realised what he'd done—'

'You were too far down to follow him back up,' Claire said.

'Thanks for rescuing him.'

'No problem.' She ruffled Ryan's hair. 'Come on, you, let's go and see the mummies.'

'Wow,' Ryan said as they walked in the front door of the British Museum a little later.

'It's the first time I've been here since they built the Millennium Court,' Claire said, staring up at the delicate trelliswork in the ceiling. 'It's stunning.'

Not as stunning as *you*, Eliot thought. He couldn't resist sliding his arm round her shoulders again as she led them through to the Egyptian section. 'My parents brought me here when I was about his age,' Claire said. 'I think he'll enjoy this.'

Ryan went from case to case, exclaiming over every new find. 'Daddy, these were Egyptian mummies from a hundred days ago!'

'Timing,' Eliot muttered to Claire with a grin.

'Jed can't tell the difference between last week, yesterday and a thousand years ago either,' she said, returning the smile.

'And, look, here's a cat. And a crocodile! And look at this writing, it's all in pictures!' Ryan squeaked.

Claire couldn't resist buying him a book about hieroglyphics and a figure of an Egyptian cat in the museum gift shop. He pored over the book for most of the way home, then fell asleep in the sudden way that children did, slumping against his father.

'Oh, bless, he's shattered,' Claire said.

'And he's had a fantastic day. Thanks to you,' Eliot said.

'And you. You planned it with me,' Claire reminded him.

'I would never have brought him on my own, just in case he couldn't cope with the crowds—he doesn't like lots of people being around. And then there was the escalator. I knew something like that would happen.'

'He was fine. It's an easy mistake to make, and he'll learn from it for next time.'

There was going to be a next time? Pleasure surged through Eliot's veins.

'As for the crowds, he had too much to think about to worry about other people.'

'Yeah. I guess there's some truth in the ''paranoid parent'' label,' Eliot said ruefully.

'You're not paranoid. Just concerned.'

'Thanks for the vote of confidence.'

Their gazes met and held. *Tell her*, Eliot thought. Tell her how you feel about her. But he knew he couldn't. If she didn't feel the same, he'd lose her completely. And it was better to have her in his life as a friend than not at all.

*   *   *

When they got back to Birmingham, Eliot carried Ryan from the train and gently put him in the car, strapping his seat belt on. They drove back to Ludbury in near silence. Eliot couldn't trust himself to speak in case he blurted out the truth. That he loved Claire, wanted her in his life properly, wanted to be a family with her.

Claire, for her part, was content to relax in the passenger seat, listening to the Vivaldi cello concerto Eliot had put on the car stereo system and enjoying his nearness. Today had changed things somehow. The hand-holding, the way he'd slid his arm round her shoulders. It had felt so *right*. Her head knew that it was a bad move, that it could never work between them, but for once she was going to go with her heart rather than her head.

Eliot parked outside Claire's house.

'Thanks for the lift home,' she said.

'Thanks for such a brilliant day.'

'I enjoyed it,' she said simply.

'Me, too.'

'Eliot...'

'Claire...' They both spoke at once.

'You first,' Eliot said.

'No. It was nothing.' She wasn't going to push things too fast. Let them go at their own pace. 'What were you going to say?'

'Can't remember.'

His face was very close to hers. So close that she could see his eyes, see the way his pupils had grown huge. She knew what was going to happen next. Knew it in her bones. Knew she should back away right now, thank him for the lift and get out of the car before…

Too late. His mouth touched hers. Lightly. No demands. Just a gentle, questioning touch.

And then her hands were round his neck, her fingers tangled in his hair. Her lips opened beneath his and he deepened the kiss, exploring the sweetness of her mouth.

The fireworks started all over again. Mad, crazy bursts of colour. She had no idea how long the kiss went on—a few seconds, minutes?—but when it finally ended, she was shaking.

'Um. That was meant to be a—' he began.

'Shh.' She placed her finger against his lips. Bad move. He sucked the tip of her finger into his mouth and a shiver of pure pleasure ran down her spine.

'Not fair. I can't think straight when you do that,' she murmured.

'Me neither. Not when you're this close.'

'We're supposed to be just good friends.'

'We *are*.'

'That wasn't a friendly kiss.'

He grinned. 'It wasn't *un*friendly.'

She stroked his face. 'We're not supposed to be doing this.'

He swivelled slightly so he could press a kiss into her palm. 'Stop touching me, then.'

'Um.' She pulled herself together with an effort. 'It's not sensible. It's too complicated. And we have to consider Ryan.'

'I know.'

'And I'm your boss.'

'I know.' He moved her hand from his face, then kissed the pulse in her wrist. 'And if you don't go indoors now, I think I'm going to embarrass us both.'

'So what are we going to do about this?'

'Um...' He pulled her into his arms and kissed her again.

'We're in your car,' she pointed out when he let her up for air.

'Behaving like teenagers.' He nibbled at her lower lip.

'Behaving like people half our age.' She kissed him back, revelling in the touch and taste of him.

'Your neighbours are going to talk.'

She grinned. Right at that moment, she couldn't have cared less. 'Uh-huh.'

'Hopeless. You're meant to be the older, sensible one.'

'Which makes you a flighty toyboy.'

He kissed her again. 'Now, there's a thought.'

'So what are we going to do?'

'I have a few suggestions.' He nuzzled the side of her face. 'But definitely not in my car, in front of my sleeping child and whoever's twitching a curtain over there.'

'You have a point.' She pulled back. 'Eliot… We're going to have to be sensible— at least talk about this.'

'In daylight. When we're both feeling more logical and sensible. Yep, I know.' He paused for half a heartbeat. 'Oh, hell. Right now, I don't give a damn about logic. Come here.' He leaned over and kissed her again. 'I've wanted to do this for weeks. And I don't know what your perfume is, but it drives me crazy.'

'Addict, by Dior,' she said.

'That figures.' He kissed her again. 'Claire Thurman, I think I could get addicted to you, given the chance.'

'Could you, now?'

'Mmm-hmm.' He tilted his head back. 'Kiss me, Claire. Please?'

Just as she leaned forward, there was a murmur from the back seat.

The moment shattered. 'Ryan,' she whispered. 'He needs you. You'd better get him home to bed.'

'We'll talk. Tomorrow,' Eliot promised. 'We'll work this out. Somehow.'

The next morning, Claire was on the early shift and didn't get a chance to speak to Eliot before she went to work. Then a call came from the maternity ward. 'Claire, we've got a twenty-seven-weeker. We can't stop labour. We've given her steroids to help the baby's lungs but she's going to deliver now.'

'I'm on my way,' Claire said.

'Please, please, don't let me lose my baby,' Mandy Knights gabbled hysterically between contractions. 'It's my fault. I should have taken it easier. Please. I don't want my baby to die.

And my husband's not here. I don't want to have my baby without him here!'

'We're all doing our best,' Claire told her gently, holding her hand. 'Has anyone called your husband?'

She nodded. 'I rang him when my waters broke. Colin's an architect—he's on some site in the middle of Scotland. Oh, lord, he's in the middle of nowhere and our baby's three months too early!'

'Is he on his way?' Claire asked gently.

'He said he's getting a plane to Birmingham and a taxi here.'

'Then I'm sure he won't be too long,' Claire reassured her. 'He might even be here by the time the baby arrives. And there's a lot we can do to help when your baby's born. Do you know if you're having a boy or a girl?'

Mandy nodded. 'A boy. We're going to call him Robbie. After Robbie Williams—one of his songs was playing when we found out the IVF had worked. You know, "Angels"? It was so perfect, I cried.'

'Course you did.' If Claire had ever done a pregnancy test of her own and seen a blue line there, she would have bawled her eyes out, too. Claire squeezed Mandy's hand. 'Robbie will need to come up to the special care baby unit because he's so small and so young, but you and Colin will be able to spend as much time as you like with him, holding his hand and talking to him. Robbie will need a lot of monitoring equipment to help us keep an eye on him, but I'll take you through it all when we're on the ward. He'll need to be fed through a vein because he's too young to suck and swallow at the same time as breathing—but we can talk through the feeding options upstairs, and whether you want him to have your own milk.'

'I never thought I'd have a baby of my own. Not after Nigel...' The woman swallowed. 'My former partner. He gave me chlamydia and I didn't know. I didn't have any symptoms.'

Claire felt her palms grow clammy. No. She didn't want to hear this. She really, really didn't want to hear this. It was way, way too close to home. But she couldn't walk out now and ask someone else to deal with her patient. Not without an explanation she didn't want to give—besides, she was the best-qualified person in the hospital to look after this baby. She couldn't let Mandy down.

'By the time I found out, my tubes were too damaged and they told me there was no way I'd ever be able to fall pregnant. Then he left me so he could have a baby with someone else. I hated him for it—I hated him so much.'

Oh, yes. Claire knew that feeling well. Bitterness and hurt and anger all mixed in. Why me? What have I done to deserve this? Why didn't I have any idea? Why, why, why didn't I have any symptoms? And how can he still have a family when I can't?

'And then I met Colin and knew he was the one. I tried to break it off with him—I knew it wasn't fair, tying him down to me when I knew he wanted kids and I couldn't have them. But he said he didn't care, he wanted me and nothing else mattered.'

Was that what Eliot would say, if she told him the truth about herself and Paddy? Claire didn't know and she couldn't risk it. It slammed home to her with full force. The kissing, the new turn in their relationship—it all had to stop. Right now. Because what she was doing wasn't fair to anyone.

'Then I got broody.'

Tell me about it, Claire thought. Every time I see one of my mums go home with her tiny baby, I wonder what it'd be like.

'We decided to try IVF and it took us four cycles—the last one was our last chance and I was so scared. And when we found out it had worked… Colin wanted to wrap me in cotton wool but I just wanted to be a normal mum. That's all I wanted, to be like other mums. And now…' Mandy broke off on a sob. 'Please, please, don't let us lose our baby now.'

'Hey. First of all, it's highly unlikely that you went into labour early because you'd been overdoing it. What do you do?'

'I'm a computer programmer.'

'So you don't have to stand for long periods—that's one thing that's been linked with premature delivery. That's good. And Colin's been supportive during your pregnancy?'

'Yes, of course. This is *our* baby. This business trip was going to be his last one until the baby arrives. He said once I reached thirty weeks he wasn't going to leave my side.' A tear streaked down Mandy's cheek. 'It wasn't supposed to be like this. I'm not supposed to be here. This can't be happening.'

Claire stroked her hand. 'You've been to all your antenatal appointments, and with an IVF baby you've been even more carefully monitored than the average mum. And my guess is that you don't smoke.'

'And I've eaten properly, haven't touched a drop of alcohol since before we started trying for IVF.'

'See? You've done your bit perfectly. You've cut out all the known risks for early delivery. And, frankly, if you had to spend your whole pregnancy sitting around with your feet up, eating chocolates, you'd be bored out of your mind, you'd be extremely unhealthy because you'd had no exercise, and you'd have the delivery from hell because you were completely unfit.'

'So it's not my fault that he's early?'

'No,' Claire reassured her. 'Though we won't necessarily know why your waters broke early. It might be that you had an infection of some sort. And *that* isn't your fault either.'

'I wanted him to be here for the birth. Colin. He should be here to see our son,' Mandy sobbed.

'I know. But if he gets delayed, it doesn't matter. We can take a photograph the moment he's born, so Colin won't miss out on seeing his newborn son,' Claire promised.

When Robbie finally arrived—before Colin had managed to reach the delivery room—Claire checked the tiny little body.

'Is he all right?' Mandy's voice quivered.

'Ten toes, ten fingers, all the bits in the right place,' Claire reassured her. 'Although he won't look quite how you were expecting, I promise you he's perfectly normal for his stage of development.'

'His head's so big,' Mandy said in horror when she saw her son.

'That's perfectly normal for this stage,' Claire repeated. 'The soft hair on his body is called lanugo, and it will fall off naturally during the next three months. His skin's very thin, which is why you can see the blood vessels underneath, but as he gets older his skin will thicken and he won't look so purple. The wrinkles are just because he hasn't had time to put any fat on yet.'

'And he's got no eyelashes,' Mandy breathed.

'He's beautiful,' Claire said.

'Why isn't he crying?'

'He's too young,' Claire explained. 'He'll sleep for most of the day, and he won't move very much because he doesn't have much muscle tone yet.'

Mandy met her eyes. 'Is he going to die?'

'He's got a good chance of surviving—he's nearly three pounds in weight, and around eighty per cent of babies born at twenty-seven weeks do survive. He'll need a fairly long stay on my ward, though, and the first seventy-two hours are the most critical,' Claire warned. 'I'm going to take him upstairs now, and as soon as Eve has checked you over, you can come up and I'll introduce you to the nurse who'll be looking after Robbie.'

She transferred the baby to the crib and headed upstairs with her precious charge. As she neared the ward, her heart grew heavier. Eliot was bound to call her at the ward, maybe take her out for lunch so they could talk. But she knew there was nothing to talk about. There never could be an 'us'. Seeing Mandy had brought home all too clearly what could happen with her own life. She couldn't put Eliot through all that worry and pain. She'd step back a bit, be his friend, until he found someone who deserved to share his life, his life and Ryan's.

And if her heart was breaking in the meantime... She'd just have to deal with it.

CHAPTER SEVEN

'LET me guess. SBCU on a Sunday morning... You're either doing paperwork or you're rushed off your feet,' Eliot said.

'Both,' Claire said wryly. She could almost hear his smile down the phone.

'Then here's the deal. Ryan and I will make you a picnic—I know it's pouring with rain, but we can have it in my car. In the middle of the hospital car park. And that way I'll know you've had a proper break.'

He was so thoughtful and caring. No wonder she'd fallen in love with him.

And because she loved him, she had to let him go. She had to let him find someone who could give him what he needed. Someone who could give him a family for Ryan. 'I'd love to, Eliot, but I've got a very sick premmie here, and I really don't want to leave him.' It was the only excuse she knew he'd accept.

'Want me to bring you a sandwich?'

'No. Thanks, but I'll be fine. Someone's bound to do a sandwich run later.' If she saw him now, her resolve would crumble.

'See you tonight?'

'I'm not sure what time I'm going to leave tonight,' she prevaricated.

'OK. Call me if you get a chance. And I'll see you at work tomorrow.'

'OK.'

'And, Claire?'

Please. Please, don't ask me about us. Or I think I'll cry. She fought to keep her voice under control. 'Yes?'

'Hope the premmie's a fighter.'

'Me, too.'

'If anyone can get him through it, you can,' Eliot said. 'See you later.'

Six hours later, the thing Claire had feared most happened: an IVH or intraventricular haemorrhage. Bleeding in the brain affected up to fifty per cent of premature babies; the earlier the baby was, the more likely it was that the bleeding would be severe.

She'd monitored Robbie's blood pressure and blood gases carefully, knowing that a bleed often didn't have any clinical signs. But when the baby suddenly went limp and unresponsive, she checked his anterior fontanelle— the soft spot at the back of his head. To her horror, it was tense, telling her that the bleed was a large one which had made the ventricles or fluid-filled spaces in his brain expand.

An ultrasound scan showed it was a large IVH. Claire fast-bleeped the neurosurgeon, who arrived just as Robbie started to have a fit.

'What's the CSF pressure?' Mac Donnelly asked. The higher the level of cerebrospinal fluid pressure, the worse the outlook.

'Twelve centimetres. I've measured his head and ventricular size,' Claire said. 'He's fitting so drugs aren't going to be enough to drain the fluid.'

'We'll use a ventriculo-peritoneal shunt,' Mac said. 'Come on, little one. Fight for us.'

But by the early evening, little Robbie had had enough. Claire had the task of breaking the news to Mandy and Colin Knights. She took them into her office.

'I'm so sorry,' she said. 'The haemorrhage was a big one. He's trying hard, but he's getting very tired now.' Her voice cracked and she took a deep breath, trying her best to sound calm and professional. The last thing the Knights needed was for her to break down, too. 'I'm so sorry. He's not going to make it.'

'Can we—can we hold him while he, he…?' Mandy's voice broke off.

'Of course you can. We'll turn the ventilator off and he can just go quietly, with his mum and dad holding him.' Claire was having a hard time keeping her own tears back. 'I'm so sorry. I know how precious he is to you.' The child they'd thought they'd never have. Their miracle baby, theirs for only a day.

She took them through to their tiny son. 'I'll be in my office if you want to talk to me or go through anything. And I can arrange for a priest to come and baptise him first, if you like.'

They both nodded, clearly too choked to speak.

Claire hated baptisms on her ward. She really, really hated them, because they were nearly always the beginning of the end and meant that the parents would be heartbroken. This one was no exception. And by the time she got home, late that evening, she was utterly drained.

Even a run with Bess didn't help much. Afterwards, she sat on her kitchen floor and howled into the dog's soft fur. Vi made no comment about Claire's red-rimmed eyes when she returned the dog, simply saying, 'I've put the kettle on.'

'Thanks, but I'm fine.'

Vi raised an eyebrow. 'Work?'

'Yeah. We lost a little one today,' Claire admitted. 'It's always hard.'

'I'd better make that a brandy, then.'

Claire shook her head. 'I'm fine. Really. I just need a hot bath and a good sleep.' She ruffled Bess's fur. 'And it helped, going for a run with madam.' Not much, but she didn't want to worry Vi any further.

A shower didn't help. Neither did the half-tub of premium ice cream in the top of her freezer. She thought about phoning Eliot, but hung up before she'd dialled half his number. What would she say, anyway? *We lost the baby. And I'm upset because it could have been me. Could have been us.* And then all the explanations... No. She couldn't face it.

The phone rang and she let the answering-machine take the call. She wasn't in the mood for talking to anyone.

'Hi, it's me. I've just spoken to Dee. She told me about little Robbie Knights. I'm so sorry. Come over when you get in. I'll make you hot chocolate and cinnamon toast.' Eliot. Tall, strong, dependable Eliot. Offering comfort. And how she needed comfort right now. Someone to hold her and tell her everything was going to be all right.

Leave it. Just leave it, she warned herself. But her hand wasn't listening and neither was her mouth.

She picked up the receiver. 'Hello?'

'Claire. You OK? No, that's a stupid question. Of course you're not. Come over,' he urged.

'I'm OK.'

'No, you're not. Nobody is when they lose a littlie. If you don't feel like driving, I'll send a taxi over for you.'

'Thanks, but I'll be fine. I just need some sleep.' Because if I come over, I'm going to cry. I'm going to tell you about Mandy's chlamydia—and then I'm going to tell you about me. The truth. And that will be the end of everything. I don't want to see the pity in your eyes. Or the embarrassment when you realise I can't give you what you need, what Ryan needs, and you want to back off but don't know how to tell me. I just can't face it. 'See you on the ward tomorrow.'

'All right. Though remember I'm here if you want to talk.'

She didn't. And Eliot noticed it when he walked onto the ward next morning. Claire was her usual professional self, but her smile didn't reach her eyes. The shutters were down and the gate was guarded by a dragon.

He knew she was upset about losing little Robbie—a death in a special care baby unit reminded everyone just how fragile these babies were, and how easily any of them could give up the fight—but it seemed to have hit Claire particularly hard. As if there was something personal about it.

'Come on. I'll shout you lunch,' he said.

'Thanks, but I'm up to my eyes in paperwork. I'll stick to a sandwich at my desk.'

He frowned. 'Have I said something to upset you? Done anything? *Not* done something? Because if I have, I apologise unreservedly. Just tell me so I don't do it again.'

She shook her head. 'I'd just rather be on my own right now. That's all.'

'Look, Claire, if you're blaming yourself for losing Robbie Knights, don't. It was a huge IVH, from what Mac said. You couldn't have done anything more than you did to save him.'

'Yeah.'

There was something else, something she wasn't telling him. He knew it in his bones. And he also knew that she wasn't ready to talk about it. If he pushed her now, it would backfire spectacularly. As for talking about the change in their relationship... He had to take it softly, slowly, coax her round. Teach her that she could trust him. 'You're a good doctor, Claire,' he said quietly. 'The best. I've learned a lot, working with you.'

'Thanks.'

The smile was definitely limited to her mouth. And her eyes were warning him not to push her any further. Eliot decided to be sensible and take heed of the warning signs. 'See you later.'

But Claire was still brooding a week later. She'd turned down Eliot's invitations to go roller-skating and explore a castle at the weekend, claiming that she was working on a research proposal, and she'd only seen Ryan once during the week, at Ally's. A gradual withdrawal, she promised herself. She had to make a gradual withdrawal from Eliot and his son. It was best for all of them. Even though it hurt like hell. Because they weren't her family, never could be. Prolonging this was just prolonging the torture, for all of them.

And then she saw the shadows under Eliot's eyes when he came on his shift on the Tuesday morning.

'Is Ryan OK?' she asked, sure that only worry about Ryan could have made him look that drained.

'Yes.'

Short, to the point of being rude—that wasn't like Eliot. She frowned. 'Are *you* all right?'

'Fine.'

Clearly he wasn't. And although she couldn't fault his work that morning, or his care and attention to their tiny patients and their parents, she knew his mind was elsewhere. That he was sick with worry. That someone had to make him talk. And that she was that someone.

At lunchtime, she tapped him on the shoulder. 'Come on. Sandwich. My shout.'

'I don't need a sandwich.'

'Yes, you do. It's your lunch-break. And don't you dare tell me you've got paperwork. I'll pull rank,' she threatened.

That earned her half a smile. But at least he gave in and walked to the canteen with her.

They bought sandwiches and wandered out into the hospital gardens. Claire chose a quiet spot beneath a tree, sat down and patted the grass beside her. 'So what's happened?' she asked.

'Says the woman who's been quiet for a week and won't tell me what's wrong.'

'Hormones?'

As excuses went, it ranked alongside washing her hair. From the old-fashioned look he gave her, he knew it, too. She considered herself lucky that he didn't press the point.

'Tell me about it, Eliot,' she said gently.

He drew his knees up to his chin, wrapping his arms round his legs. 'I got a letter from Malandra's solicitor yesterday. Apparently, she's remarried. And she wants custody of Ryan.'

'What? After more than five years of no contact whatsoever?' Claire stared at him in disbelief. 'Why?'

He shrugged. 'Dunno.'

'But you've got a theory.' She could tell from the set look on his face.

He grimaced. 'Let's just say that my parents left Ryan a decent trust fund.'

'And you think she wants to get her hands on the money?'

'Not her—she never used to be like that, anyway. It's the new husband. According to some of our old friends, he's looking to recoup his losses on the stock market. Getting control of a trust fund...well. It'd solve his problems, wouldn't it?'

'It won't happen.'

'Won't it?' Eliot raised an eyebrow. 'Malandra's his mother. She can offer Ryan a stable home.'

'You're his father. And Ryan's *got* a stable home.'

'One parent, plus a childminder,' he reminded her. 'And my track record with childminders hasn't exactly been brilliant, has it?'

'Fran was young and if she hadn't met that particular boyfriend, she might have been perfect for Ryan.'

'She wasn't. I just wanted her to be, because I was desperate. Oh, hell. What if they give Malandra custody?'

'They won't,' Claire reassured him. 'Anyone who knows you can tell how much you love Ryan. You've cared for him on your own for over five years, and you've made a great job of it. He's a happy, healthy, well-adjusted child and he loves you. No judge would take him away from you.'

'I can't risk it, Claire. So I'm sorry—I'll have to hand my notice in.'

'Eliot, you can't. You love what you do and you're doing a great job—in fact, if Kelly decides not to come back after her maternity leave, I was thinking of asking you to stay on permanently. And the hospital board agrees with me.'

'Ryan needs me.'

'I know, but your job isn't the issue here.'

'How else can I prove I'm looking after him perfectly, unless I'm doing it full time?' He shook his head. 'I was awake all night, thinking about it. And the only other—' He broke off. 'No.'

'Only other what?' she prompted.

'The only other option,' he said tonelessly, 'is for me to be in the same position as Malandra. Married. So I can offer Ryan a stable home with two parents.'

Married. Eliot, *married*. Well, he had a point. It would be good for him, and for Ryan. Hadn't she already thought all that through, worked out that he needed to find someone who really suited him and promised herself she wouldn't stand in his way?

So why did the idea of Eliot marrying someone else make her feel as if someone were dissecting her heart with a rusty knife?

'Completely mad.'

'What?' She'd missed most of what he was saying.

'I said, at three o'clock this morning I thought of the perfect solution, but it was completely mad. You'll say no so there's no point in asking.'

'No to what?' she asked, mystified.

'Marrying me.'

No down-on-one-knee, no declaration of love, no nothing. He didn't even look as if he was saying something out of the ordinary. No, he probably hadn't even *said* that. It had been a mixture of wishful thinking and...

She blinked, hoping to clear her head. 'Did you just ask me to marry you?'

She looked shocked. No, worse than shocked. Disgusted. Eliot could have howled with frustration and anger at himself. He'd just made the most stupid mistake of his life. Claire was the one person who could have helped him see a way through all this mess, and he'd done the one thing guaranteed to make her run a mile.

It had to be sleep deprivation. That was the only reason why he'd let his mouth run away with him. Of course she wasn't going to marry him.

He'd already worked out that she'd been married before, that her ex-husband had hurt her badly. An affair, he guessed, judging by the way she'd reacted to Estée, their patient whose baby had had rhesus haemolytic disease. So marriage wouldn't be top of her favourite subjects. Plus he knew that she didn't want children of her own, and marrying him meant taking on a seven-year-old stepson with special needs.

And yet…something didn't quite add up.

Claire didn't dislike children. She had a godson she adored; she'd offered to spend time with Ryan over the past few weeks and they'd clearly both enjoyed themselves; she'd rescued Ryan on the escalator without being irritated; and then there was look on her face sometimes when she made a fuss over one of the babies on the ward.

So why didn't she want children of her own? Had she miscarried, or lost a tiny baby, and was scared that she'd have to go through the same thing again? Was that why Robbie Knights's death had hit her so hard?

And then a really nasty thought hit him. Maybe it wasn't children—maybe it wasn't even the thought of marriage. Maybe he'd simply misread all the signs. He'd fallen for her so hard, he'd thought that if he loved her enough she would love him, too. How stupid could he get?

'Forget I said anything. I told you it was completely mad.'

'Hang on. You ask me to marry you—and you expect me just to ignore it?'

'I'm not thinking straight.'

'Too right, you're not thinking straight. No way would we be able to convince a judge that it wasn't a marriage of convenience. Look at the timing. Yesterday you get a letter saying your ex-wife wants custody and today you're planning your wedding. QED—this marriage isn't a real one. It's a reaction fuelled by panic.' She rolled her eyes. 'It's obvious to anyone, Eliot.'

We. She'd said 'we'. Did that mean…? Hope flared for a brief, bright, painful second. And then died. Of course not.

'Do you really think that being married would make a difference, make a judge think you were a better parent?' she continued.

'Ryan would have two parents. That means a stable home,' Eliot said. 'It means I have back-up. If one of us can't be there for him, the other one will be. Whereas now it's me or a childminder—and if the childminder can't help me out, I'm completely stuck.'

'And your lawyer thinks…?'

'The same.' Eliot spread his hands. 'I mean, he didn't say it in so many words, but he said that Malandra has a case. If she can prove she had postnatal depression which made her reject her son but she's recovered now and wants the child she carried for nine months—what judge is going to say no?'

'Access,' Claire said crisply. 'The solution would be to let her have access. If she takes

Ryan away from you, she's going to introduce an enormous change into his life—his home, his routine, everything. Does she live near here?'

'No.'

'So he'd have to change schools as well. A new home, a new town, a new school—it'll be too much for him. Children with Asperger's don't cope well with change, so the medics are all going to be batting for you and saying that you need to keep his routine exactly as it is.'

'But supposing that's not enough of an argument? Supposing it's more important for him to be with his mother? I don't want to take the risk. The more I think about it, the more I realise it has to be marriage, Claire.' He raked a hand through his hair. 'It doesn't have to be permanent—just long enough to convince a judge that the best place for Ryan is with me.'

'It's a pretty cynical reason to get married—to keep your son.'

'And insulting to you.' He couldn't bring himself to meet her gaze. 'It's obvious what I'd get out of it. What would you get out of a temporary marriage to a junior doctor with no prospects and a son with special needs?'

* * *

You, Claire thought. I'd get you.

She'd already dreamed about it and dismissed it. If Eliot was married to her, he wouldn't be able to look for someone who'd suit him properly. Someone who could be a real wife to him, who could give him a brother or sister for Ryan and make their family complete. Yes, they could do what Mandy and Colin Knights had done and seek IVF treatment, but that needed a lot of strength, a lot of time, and it wouldn't be fair to Ryan. The little boy had special needs, so he had to come first. IVF simply wasn't an option.

But what Eliot had just said changed everything. *It doesn't have to be permanent.* A temporary marriage. The three of them, together, as a proper family. It could be hers for a while, just for long enough to store up some good memories for the years ahead. She could have what she wanted, just for a little while, without ruining their lives. It was tempting. So very tempting.

Her common sense muscled in. Eliot hadn't said anything about loving her. They were friends—good friends—and there was a definite attraction between them. Was friendship and attraction enough of a basis for marriage?

Then again, she'd been in love with Paddy. Deeply, passionately in love. And all the love in the world hadn't been enough to keep her marriage intact.

She weighed up the options. If she said no, she might be wiping out Eliot's last hopes of keeping his son. If she said yes... 'How long have you got to work something out?'

'I don't know. However long these things take to get to court. And if Malandra's new husband can call in some favours and get the case bumped up the lists...' He shrugged. 'I suppose I'd better get used to the idea of losing my son.'

'Have you said anything to Ryan about it?'

Eliot shook his head. 'To be honest, I've chickened out of saying anything to him about his mother. I don't want him to think she abandoned him because she didn't love him or because he's a bit different. I'm not going to lie to him and say she's dead, but how do I explain why she didn't want to see him? He never talks about her, never seems to notice that we're not like his friends at school. So I've avoided the issue.' He sighed. 'Which is going to make things a hundred times worse now. But I never dreamed she'd change her mind. Not after all this time.'

'How would he feel about you getting married?'

'It depends who I was marrying.'

'And when you say a temporary arrangement…'

This time Eliot looked at her. 'You'd really consider it?'

'I'm not seeing anyone and I've been married before, so a temporary marriage isn't going to spoil any dreams of hearts and flowers and walking up the aisle in a floaty dress. You and I are friends, and Ryan and I get on well together. So, actually, asking me to marry you temporarily is logical.' The fact that I'm in love with you… Well, that's a complication you don't need to know, she thought.

'You'd really do that for me?'

'If our positions were reversed—say, I was the single parent and I needed to get married to stop my ex taking our child away—would you marry me temporarily?'

'Of course I would.'

'Well, then. Provided it's OK with Ryan, let's do it. And we'd better, um, talk practicalities.'

*   *   *

Claire was going to marry him. *Claire was going to marry him!* He wanted to pull her to her feet, whoop, whirl her round, kiss her senseless...

No. She was doing this as a friend. Nothing more. So from now on he was going to have to keep his hands to himself. Friends. Good friends.

And then a sneaky thought crept in. Maybe once they were married, once they were living together, she'd learn to love him. And maybe he could persuade her to make their marriage permanent...

'Well?'

'Sorry. I didn't hear a word of what you said. I'm just trying to take in the fact you said yes.'

'It's what any friend would do.'

Friend. Not lover. She was completely upfront about it, so why was his heart refusing to listen to her?

'So, your place or mine?'

Anywhere. No. She's talking about where you're going to live. Not what you'd *like* her to be talking about, he told himself sharply. 'Um. To keep Ryan's routine as normal as possible, it should be mine. I'll, um, take the sofa.' His terrace only had two bedrooms, one Ryan's. Even the idea of sharing a bedroom—a *bed*—with Claire strained his self-control. The reality would break it completely.

'OK. I'll rent my place out in the meantime.'

How could she possibly discuss this so calmly? Because, a little voice in his head reminded him, *she's* not in love with *you*.

'When should we…um, set the date?'

'There's not much point in waiting.'

'I'll ring the register office this afternoon, see when they've got a slot free.' They were planning their wedding, discussing it as if it were just another day in their lives. This, Eliot thought, was surreal. 'What about a reception?'

'We'll throw a party later. When the court case is over.'

A divorce party, not a wedding party. 'And you think the ward will be OK with that?'

'Cake and champagne should do it. We'll say we wanted to keep it small and quiet for Ryan.'

'I don't have any family,' he reminded her. 'So it'd be just your family and some close friends.'

'OK.' She stood up. 'Um, perhaps I should come over tonight, so we can talk to Ryan about it? And then we'll work out what we need to do.'

They could have been discussing a conference or a research proposal—not their wedding, Eliot thought ruefully. But, then, he'd been the one to suggest it. He'd been the one to state the terms. A temporary marriage, based on friendship, until the court case was resolved.

And there was only one way he'd kiss her as he carried her over the threshold. In his dreams.

CHAPTER EIGHT

'ARE you sure you're doing the right thing?' Ally asked.

Claire smiled. From the moment she'd called Ally at the crèche and asked to meet her in the coffee-shop just down the road from the hospital after work, she'd known that her best friend would interrogate her. And she had her answers off pat. 'Yes. Eliot has to be able to offer Ryan as much as his mother can: a stable home with two parents.'

'But if you're not in love with each other...'

'I've been there, done that, and got my fingers burned,' Claire reminded her. Though even Ally didn't know quite how far Paddy's betrayal had gone.

Ally dipped her chocolate swizzle stick in her latte. 'And you don't think you're going to get burned this time round? Come on, you can't base a marriage on friendship. There's got to be attraction there as well.'

Claire simply shrugged. Of course there was. But how could she act on that attraction?

She wasn't going to be Eliot's wife for always—only until the custody issue had been resolved. For all their sakes, they had to stick to friendship, a marriage in name only.

Ally finished her chocolate and gave Claire a knowing look. 'I heard Ryan telling Jed that you were holding hands with his dad when you went to London. That's not what friends do. So are you going to tell me what's really going on?'

Claire spent a very long time on her own chocolate swizzle stick. Ally waited patiently. In the end, Claire gave in. She should have known she couldn't hide it from Ally. 'All right, I admit it. I find him attractive.' Everything about him. His face, his eyes, his mouth, his body, the way he smiled, his sense of humour—everything. To the point of having X-rated fantasies about him. Fantasies she knew she could never, ever live out.

'But you don't think he feels the same way about you?'

Yes. No. Maybe. She didn't know. 'It's complicated. Like I said, I'm marrying him to help him out. As his friend. Temporarily, until he's got custody of Ryan assured.'

'I see. And you think you're going to be able to convince a judge this is a real marriage when you're really just good friends.' It was a statement more than a question.

'We have to.'

'And then you're going to get divorced.'

'Yes.'

Ally frowned. 'It doesn't make any sense. And what about Ryan? What happens to him when you get divorced?'

'I'll still see him. Still be his friend.'

'And when Eliot finds someone else?'

She'd been trying not to think about that. Not to feel. Because although she knew it would be the right thing for him, to find someone who could give him everything he needed—someone who could give him everything she couldn't—it was a day she dreaded. The day when she would have to smile and smile and wish him all the best, when inside her heart would be shredding into tiny irreparable pieces at his loss. 'I'll fade into the background. Gradually. So Ryan doesn't get hurt.'

'You,' Ally said, 'are going to get hurt. Badly. Don't do it.'

'I promised I would.'

'Tell him you've thought about it and realised you're making a mistake.'

'I'm not making a mistake, Ally.'

Ally frowned. 'Please, tell me you're not hoping that once you're married, Eliot will fall in love with you and it'll all work out.'

'Of course I'm not,' Claire lied.

Ally didn't look convinced, but she didn't press the point. 'OK. So have you set a date yet?'

'Next Monday. Provided Ryan's OK with it.'

'When are you going to tell him?'

'Tonight.'

'Right.' Ally paused. 'And you've got a dress sorted out? A going-away outfit? A honeymoon?'

'No honeymoon, no going-away outfit, and I've got a nice suit that'll do for the register office.'

'A nice suit?' Ally curled her lip. 'Absolutely not. You're not getting married in a work outfit, Claire Thurman.' She lowered her voice. 'Even if it isn't going to be a proper marriage, you're going to look fantastic on your wedding day.'

'I did the big floaty dress thing last time,' Claire reminded her.

'I know, and no one expects you to do that this time. Especially at a small, quiet wedding. But you and I are going late-night shopping on Thursday night to find you a wedding dress.' Ally raised her eyebrows. 'It's the duty of the matron of honour to make sure the bride looks fabulous.'

'I didn't think you had a matron of honour at a civil wedding.'

'You're having one, for this one,' Ally said.

'I can't. I'm on a late on Thursday.'

'That's a feeble excuse. Swap shifts.'

'I'm not going to get out of this, am I?' Claire asked wryly.

'Course you're not. I'll do your hair, and Ed's sister Kim will do your make-up—yes, I know you can do it perfectly well yourself, but I think a wedding deserves the professional touch, don't you?'

'But, Ally—'

'No buts. If you're going to do something this crazy, you're going to do it in style. And that's an end to it.'

Claire smiled. 'OK, I give in. Thank you. We'll go dress-shopping on Thursday.'

'And when it's picking-up-the-pieces time,' Ally said softly, reaching over to squeeze her hand, 'I'll be here.'

Claire knew she meant it. Ally had been there for her last time, when she'd discovered that all Paddy's promises had been so much piecrust. Empty and easily broken. Though Claire had been too ashamed of her final discovery to tell anyone, even Ally.

She could only hope that this time round things wouldn't be quite so messy. Though she had a nasty feeling that this time round her heart wouldn't recover. Ever.

'Hello, Claire!' Ryan beamed at her when he answered the front door an hour or so later. 'Daddy said we're having tea with you tonight.'

'Yes.' She held up the box. 'Pizza. I picked it up on the way home. And garlic bread with cheese, your favourite.'

'Cool.'

'Do you want to go and lay the table for me?'

'I've already done it.'

'How about pouring the juice?'

As the little boy sped off, she mouthed to Eliot, 'Have you told him yet?'

He shook his head. 'I thought we should do it together.'

'After we've eaten.'

Somehow she managed to get through the meal, listening to Ryan's scheme for building a rocket to go to Mars and dutifully admiring the neat sketches the little boy had added to his carefully labelled 'Rocket Plans' file.

When they'd finished eating, Eliot cleared the plates away.

'Can I go on the computer now?' Ryan asked.

'In a moment, son. There's something I want to ask you. Something important.' Eliot looked at him. 'How would you feel about Claire coming to live with us?'

'All the time?'

'All the time,' Claire confirmed. Her stomach felt as if a thousand buffalo were stampeding through it. If Ryan hated the idea, it would all be off before it started. And she'd lose her temporary family.

'Cool,' he said.

'Then Claire and I are going to get married,' Eliot said. 'Next Monday.'

'Cool. Will that make you my mummy, Claire? Like Ally's Jed's mummy?'

Claire's heart started to rip in two. *My mummy.* The words she'd never, ever thought to hear. Except she couldn't be Ryan's mummy. Her marriage to Eliot wasn't going to be a proper, for-ever-and-ever sort of marriage. 'Sort of,' she prevaricated.

'Cool. Can I go on the computer now?' Ryan asked again.

Eliot nodded, and the little boy sped off.

'Well, that was easier than I thought,' Claire said as she switched the kettle on. 'It's going to mean quite a change in his routine.'

'Not that much. It just means you'll stay here instead of going home. He adores you, Claire.'

There had been a kind of longing in the little boy's eyes when he'd asked if she would be his mummy. Or maybe she'd wanted it to be there and had just imagined it. And she would be Eliot's wife… She pushed the treacherous thought away. Same deal as the mummy business. She'd be wife in name, not reality. She had to remember that. 'Have you told him about Malandra yet?'

'One thing at a time,' Eliot said. 'Though

I've explained the situation to the school and said that no one is to pick him up without written permission from me.'

'You don't really think she'd try to snatch him, do you?'

Eliot shrugged. 'It's been five years, Claire. I don't know her any more. She walked out on him. She wants him back. And I can't take the risk that she might...'

'Hey.' She squeezed his hand. 'I wasn't criticising.'

'Sorry. I'm overreacting. Have you told your parents?' he asked.

'I thought I'd wait until we'd told Ryan. I'll ring Mum on the way home. She and Dad will come to the wedding.'

'They don't live near here, do they?'

Claire shook her head. 'They live on the coast, in Sussex. My elder brother Rich lives in London—they'll probably stay the night with him afterwards. Oh, and Rich will probably come, too.'

'It's just struck me,' Eliot said, 'how little we know about each other. You've never said much about your family.'

'Not much to tell. I get on fine with them.'

She raised an eyebrow. 'Having second thoughts?'

'No. Just having a minor panic.'

'Me, too.'

He wanted to pull her into his arms and kiss it better, but he stopped himself. Just. Focus on the practicalities, he reminded himself. That's what Claire expects from you. She's not offering more. 'No need. The wedding's all sorted, more or less,' he said. 'Three o'clock on Monday afternoon—I'm taking Ryan out of school for the afternoon so he can be part of it all. I've booked a hotel for the reception—we just need to confirm numbers on Thursday. What sort of car do you want?'

'No need. I'll drive myself. Actually, no—there's no point in having two cars there. I'll get a taxi. And I'll organise the cake and flowers.'

'I'll get the champagne for the ward.' Eliot handed her a mug of steaming coffee. 'We're going to have to tell them tomorrow, so we'd better get our cover story straight. I mean, we can't tell them the truth.' He held her gaze. 'Do we tell them we just fell in love and decided to get married?'

'Um.' Claire took refuge in her coffee. 'I hadn't really thought about it,' she mumbled.

'They know we've been out together a few times. With Ryan.'

'Uh-huh.'

Shut up. Shut up *now*. Eliot's common sense insisted. His mouth didn't listen. 'So it would probably make sense. At work, I mean. If they thought we were...' In love. At least, *he* was.

'Yes. Of course.'

'Right. So, um, do we make a big announcement together?'

'A little one, in the staffroom. The grapevine will do the rest.'

He nodded. 'That just leaves the ring. I thought we should choose it together. So I don't get a ring that reminds you too much of your...' He tailed off. Stupid. Reminding her of her ex who'd hurt her. The ex who'd hurt her so badly that she'd refused to talk about him and Eliot didn't even know his name. 'Sorry. I didn't mean to be tactless.'

'No offence taken. We have to sort the practical things,' Claire said. 'Something plain will be fine.'

'Right. We'll get it tomorrow lunchtime, then?'

'Sure.'

* * *

Telling the ward was easier than Claire had expected. Afterwards, Tilly came up to her and gave her a huge hug. 'See? I *told* you Dr Right would turn up.'

'Yes.' Except they were living one huge lie. Eliot was Dr Right, in Claire's eyes, but he didn't know it. And she couldn't ever let him know it, because she wasn't the right one for him.

'You could have waited, though, and had a proper big do. But since there's this big rush…' Tilly eyed her speculatively '…are you going to be making another announcement shortly?'

That they were going to have a baby? Claire's heart contracted painfully. 'No.' It was an announcement she never would be able to make. The doctor had been very clear about that. Unless she went through a long course of IVF—and even that didn't come with a cast-iron guarantee—she could never, ever fall pregnant. 'There wasn't any reason to wait, that's all.'

'I'm really pleased for you both. He's

lovely, Claire. And I think you'll be good for each other.'

'Thanks, Tills.'

'And since you're keeping it a small family do for Ryan's sake, we want pictures. Especially of The Dress,' Tilly added. 'I assume you *are* having a dress?'

'Ally's dragging me round the shops on Thursday night,' Claire admitted.

'Good.' Tilly raised an eyebrow. 'Because if she hadn't suggested it, I would have dragged you round the shops myself. You deserve the best on your special day, Claire. The beginning of a lifetime of happiness.'

Claire forced herself to smile. If only. But it wasn't going to happen. It was temporary, she was going into it with her eyes wide open, and there was no reason at all why that little pain should start gnawing at her heart. Was there?

The rest of the week passed in a blur. Thursday's shopping trip netted the perfect dress—and Ally insisted on giving Claire an extra personal present, a set of beautiful silk underwear. 'Matron of honour's duty,' she said. 'You did the same for me, remember?'

'Yes. Though it went under a big floaty dress. And you were in love with Ed.'

Ally didn't say it, but they both knew it. Claire was in love with Eliot.

'Be happy, Claire. Even if it's just for a little while,' Ally said softly. 'Now, let's go and get some food before I embarrass us both and start howling.'

'Me, too,' Claire said, equally softly.

Friday brought tears to Claire's eyes. The moment she walked into her office, she saw the banners and ribbons strung everywhere, cut-out pictures of herself and Eliot perched on top of a cardboard wedding cake and confetti scattered on her desk and chair.

'You didn't think you'd get away with it, did you?' Tilly asked with a grin.

'I…just wasn't expecting this.'

'You should see what we've done to his locker,' Tilly said with a wicked look.

L-plates plus a string of old boots and tin cans taped to the front of it. Claire couldn't help laughing.

And her laughter almost turned to tears at the end of the day when Tilly presented them both with some gorgeous crystal glasses and some gift vouchers on behalf of the ward—along with an enormous pile of cards. It seemed as if everyone in the hospital had sent a card and good wishes for their marriage.

How could they lie to everyone like this?

But they had to, for Ryan's sake. And it wasn't a complete lie, she thought. She did love Eliot. And she'd be there for him during their temporary marriage.

On Saturday Eliot took Ryan out while she packed. On Sunday she and Eliot moved her personal things over to his house and got her place ready for the tenant the agency had lined up to move into Claire's house.

And suddenly it was Monday afternoon. Her wedding day.

Eliot glanced at his watch for the fifteenth time in as many seconds. How come time had slowed down almost to the point of going backwards? But that was just worry talking. Of course Claire wasn't going to be late. She was never late. And if she'd changed her mind, she would have called him and told him.

And then his mouth dried as the door opened and she walked in. She hadn't said a word about what she'd intended to wear, and he'd been expecting her to look exactly as she did at work, just without the white coat—a smart suit, her hair back in its customary French pleat, minimal make-up. He hadn't been expecting her hair to be up in a complicated array of coils, her nape bare and a single-strand pearl choker accenting the beautiful line of her neck. He hadn't been expecting the light but flawless make-up which emphasised her perfect Cupid's-bow mouth and eyes so dark and deep you could drown in them. He hadn't been expecting the eau-de-nil silk dress with spaghetti shoulder-straps and a bias-cut skirt that skimmed her body. Or the delicate strappy shoes. Or the simple bouquet of white roses she carried—a bouquet identical to the one he'd once bought her.

'You look stunning,' he breathed as she joined him at the registrar's desk.

'Thank you. You don't look so bad yourself,' she said.

He'd bought the new suit that morning. New shirt and tie, too. Crazy, when he knew it wasn't a proper marriage and she was only doing it as a favour to a friend. But he wanted to look good for her anyway.

And then the ceremony started. Simple, quiet, formal words that made them man and wife. He slipped the plain gold band onto her finger. Kissed her lightly when the registrar said he could. Slid his arm around her for the photographs.

'You're my mummy now,' Ryan said with satisfaction, and hugged Claire. Claire froze. *You're my mummy now.* How she wanted to be his mummy. A real mummy to him, a real wife to Eliot. But it wasn't part of the deal. She was doing him a favour, as a friend. No strings, no ties, no promises, no future.

Tears stung her eyes and she tried desperately to keep them back. Brides weren't supposed to cry on their wedding day. Even if they weren't proper brides.

Eliot must have seen her struggle, because he drew her close and kissed the tears from her lashes.

'He means well. It's not a life sentence,' he whispered into her ear.

That was the problem, Claire thought. It *wasn't* a life sentence. It was only temporary. But she forced herself to smile through the meal, smile as everyone toasted their future happiness, smile as she and Eliot cut the cake.

When she could bear it no longer, she glanced at her watch. 'Sorry to be a party-pooper but it's time we got Ryan home. School tomorrow,' she said.

'Actually, *we're* taking Ryan home with us,' Ally said, shocking her. 'He's having a sleep-over with Jed.'

'And I'm doing the school run tomorrow morning,' Ed chipped in.

Claire frowned. 'I don't understand.'

'You're staying the night here. Just the two of you. It's your wedding day, sis,' Rich said. 'I know you're not having a proper honey-moon—so this is my gift to you both. Be happy.' He handed Eliot a key. 'Look after my baby sister. She's special.'

'I know. And I will,' Eliot promised.

Claire glanced at the key. 'Honeymoon suite? But we've got work tomorrow. I can't go to work dressed like this!' And besides, Ally knew the truth. What was going on?

'There's a case upstairs,' Ally said. 'I, um, borrowed Eliot's keys because I said I wanted to leave you a surprise.'

'That's both of us,' Eliot said wryly. 'I thought you meant a bottle of champagne or something.'

'It was a ''something''.' Ally winked. 'See you two tomorrow. OK, Ryan, Jed. Back to ours now,' Ally directed, shepherding the boys towards the door with the help of Ed.

'Be happy, darling.' Claire's mother hugged her. 'This one's not like Paddy—he's for keeps,' she whispered in Claire's ear.

'And welcome to the family,' Claire's father said, shaking Eliot's hand.

'Thank you,' he said, a huge lump in his throat. If only they really *were* going to be his family. If only he really was going to be part of a family at last, not just muddling through on his own, lonely and terrified that he was making a total mess of bringing up his son.

Claire's brother hugged them both, and then they were alone.

Eliot looked at the key. 'I wasn't expecting this.'

'Me neither,' Claire admitted. 'The honeymoon suite. I feel a fraud.'

She didn't look that distressed about it. And it was their wedding night. Eliot decided to take a gamble. 'They've gone to a lot of trouble. It'd be a pity to waste it,' he said softly.

'And Rich meant well. I, um, didn't tell him or my parents the truth, about how we…' Her voice tailed off.

'Then shall we?'

Claire was silent for so long that he began to think he'd blown it. And then she nodded, and allowed him to take her arm.

When they opened the door and saw the four-poster bed, the champagne on ice on a silver tray with two crystal flutes and the beautiful bouquet of red roses, Eliot couldn't resist it.

'May as well do things properly,' he said, and picked her up. Before she could say anything, he carried her over the threshold into the room. He closed the door behind him with a kick and set her down on the bed.

'Champagne?' he asked.

She nodded. He took his jacket off and hung it over the back of a chair, then removed his tie and looped it over the top. He took the champagne from the ice-bucket, opened it and poured them each a glass.

'So. To us,' he said softly, raising his glass.

She clinked her glass against his and drank the toast.

He sat on the bed beside her. 'I've been thinking.'

'Yes?'

'We've got a little bit of unfinished business.'

'Unfinished business?' she echoed.

'Mmm. Something that maybe we ought to—' his voice deepened '—get out of our system. Before tomorrow.'

'Uh-huh.'

'Tomorrow we can go back to being friends.'

'And tonight?'

He took the glass from her fingers. 'Tonight, Mrs Slater, is our wedding night.'

CHAPTER NINE

MRS SLATER. A thrill ran through Claire at the words. She was married to Eliot. And tonight they were going to have the honeymoon they weren't supposed to have.

'And I believe it's traditional to dance together on your wedding night.'

She nodded, and let him draw her to her feet. He led her over to the CD player, picked a disc at random and set the machine playing. And then she was in his arms, dancing with him cheek to cheek.

'You look fabulous in that dress.'

'You don't scrub up so badly yourself,' she murmured.

His hand slid over the bodice to touch the bare skin on her back. 'Pure silk.'

Claire didn't trust herself to speak. Her mouth was dry and she could feel her pulse speeding up.

'It's almost a shame to do this, you look so lovely,' he murmured, 'but…' He removed a pin from her hair. And another. And another, until her glorious chestnut hair was free and spread over her shoulders.

He held her for a second at arm's length, studied her, smiled and pulled her back into his arms.

They swayed together in silence, just holding each other close. And then she felt Eliot's fingers straying towards the top of her zip. Her heart began to beat even faster. Was he going to…?

He was. In one smooth, fluid movement, he undid the zip. Pushed the straps from her shoulders. Let the dress drift to the floor.

'More silk,' he murmured, taking in her camisole top and knickers. 'Oh, and stockings!' Lace-topped hold-ups. 'Mmm. You really know how to drive a man wild, Claire Slater.' He held her closer, nuzzling her shoulder and stroking her waist.

'I think we need to even things up a bit here,' Claire said, giving in to temptation and starting to unbutton his shirt.

He gave her a lazy smile. 'Is that so?'

She returned his grin. Everything was going to be all right. 'I think so.'

He kicked off his shoes and let her unfasten his trousers. And then he picked her up again and carried her over to the bed.

'You've got macho tendencies,' she accused with a smile.

'Better believe it.' He joined her on the bed, lifted her hand and kissed each fingertip in turn. 'Tonight you're mine. All mine. And I'm feeling greedy.' He shifted so that he was kneeling over her, then bent to kiss her.

It was like that time in her office, when his mouth had caused her to see fireworks. Except this time there was nothing to interrupt them. There was nothing to stop Eliot's mouth moving lower, exploring the hollows of her neck, the dip of her collarbone. Nothing to stop his mouth sliding over the silk of her camisole until he reached the hard peak of her nipple. Nothing to stop him taking it into his mouth, through the silk, and sucking until she gasped and thrust her fingers into his hair, urging him on.

Slowly, he peeled her camisole upwards. 'Beautiful as this is, it has to go,' he said hoarsely. 'I want you, Claire. Properly. Skin to skin.'

'Yes,' she hissed, arching up to let him remove the silk camisole.

He felt so good. A hard, muscular body, a sprinkling of hair across his chest that gave a delicious friction against her skin.

He kissed her again. And then he peeled down her stockings, caressing every centimetre of skin as he slid the silk down her legs. Following it with his mouth, licking the back of her knee, nuzzling the hollows of her ankles. And then moving all the way up again, making her gasp and arch upwards.

By the time he'd finished, Claire was shaking. She made no protest when he gently lifted her so he could remove her knickers. She had no idea when he'd found the time to remove the rest of his own clothes, but then he was kneeling between her thighs and she stopped thinking, welcoming him into her body.

'Ah, Claire. I want you so badly.'

And she wanted him, too. Loved him. She could never tell him in so many words—it wouldn't be fair—but she showed him, with every touch, every move, every kiss.

The first time was quick for both of them, the weeks of pent-up tension boiling over. Eliot kissed away her tears, stroked her hair, held her close. And the gentleness turned into want, into need. This time it was slower, more tender.

'Forget tomorrow,' he whispered. 'This is for you and me. Right here, right now. Just us.'

She nodded, letting his clever mouth and hands build her up to another climax, and another. And finally they slept, held tight in each other's arms. Claire's last thought as she drifted to sleep was that this was where she belonged: with her man.

The next morning, Claire woke to find Eliot already dressed and pouring coffee.

'That smells good,' she said.

He smiled at her. 'I was just going to bring some over to you.'

'Breakfast in bed.' She looked down at the rumpled sheets, remembered how they'd got that way—realised that she was still completed naked—and flushed. 'Um, I'd better get up. We've got work and...' She stopped, aware that she was gabbling. Nervous. He was fully dressed, not just with a towel slung round his waist while he poured them a coffee before coming back to join her in bed. Did that mean that last night was over, that now they were going back to being friends?

She couldn't bear to hear it from him first. So she decided to be the one to bring it up. 'Thanks for the coffee, but I'd better get dressed before I drink it. Um, would you mind passing me my clothes and turning your back so I can go and have a shower?'

He went very still for a moment: and then he nodded. 'Of course.'

By the time she'd showered and washed her hair, Eliot had packed their wedding clothes into the small suitcase and straightened the bed.

'Thanks,' she said.

He shrugged. 'No problem.'

She sat at the table and sipped her coffee.

The silence stretched between them until it almost hurt. Claire suspected that Eliot felt as nervous as she did, judging by the toast he'd crumbled onto his plate. So what now?

She looked up and met his gaze.

'So—are we still friends?' he asked.

'We're still friends,' she confirmed. Of course. It was what they'd agreed. This was a temporary marriage between friends. And last night had been…unfinished business, which was now concluded.

By the time they arrived at work, Eliot was seriously doubting his sanity. How could he have been so stupid as to make love with Claire last night? Now he knew what it was like to touch her… Hell. He'd never get any sleep again.

The worst thing was, she clearly didn't feel the same way about him. When she'd woken, if she'd smiled at him or given him the merest inclination that she wanted him back in bed beside her, he'd have left the coffee to go cold, ripped off his clothes and to hell with work and everything else. But she hadn't. She'd asked him to turn his back while she went for a shower. Making it very clear that their honeymoon night had been just that. A night. One single, unrepeatable night. From now on their relationship was going to be strictly platonic.

And he was going to have to live with it.

'I'm sorry. I just didn't take it in—though he did explain everything to me the other day,' Sara Rivers said. 'That nice doctor. The good-looking one with lovely green eyes.'

There was only one person Sara Rivers could be talking about. Claire's skin heated as she remembered just how good-looking Eliot had been at two o'clock in the morning. Rumpled and sexy, those green eyes laughing as he'd tempted her to kiss him and...

Tilly smiled and patted Claire's shoulder. 'She's the worst person you could ask, you know.'

'But...' Sara glanced at Claire's badge. 'But you're a consultant.'

'Oh, not about medical things. She's brilliant,' Tilly hastened to explain. 'But you won't get a word of sense out of her about our Dr Slater. She got married to him yesterday. That's why she's got that daydreamy look on her face.'

'So the gorgeous slices of fruit cake by the coffee-machine are from your wedding cake? Oh!' Sara looked mortified. 'I'm so sorry, I didn't realise. Congratulations, Dr Slater. I hope you'll both be very happy.'

'Thanks. But my name's Thurman,' Claire corrected.

Sara looked surprised. 'You haven't taken his name, then?'

Claire shook her head. 'I'm known professionally as Claire Thurman—so it's easier to use that name at work.'

'Plus I suppose it'd be confusing if someone called for Dr Slater—you wouldn't know which one they meant,' Sara said.

'Something like that.' Claire wasn't bothered about titles. She believed parents had more important things to worry about than whether their consultant should be called Dr or Mrs. Plus, when her temporary marriage to Eliot was over, she wouldn't have to change her name again, as she had with Paddy. She wouldn't have to go through all the painful explanations.

Claire forced her mind back to work. 'So Eliot told you that Liam here has apnoea?'

Sara nodded. 'I—I suppose I was too shocked to take it in at the time. All I could think of is that my little boy's in Special Care, he's ill and he was born too early so I can't take him home.'

'He's in the best place right now,' Claire reassured her. 'What apnoea means is that Liam pauses in his breathing, and the pause lasts for more than fifteen or twenty seconds. He might look blue or pale, and his heart rate

will slow to less than eighty beats a minute—
what we call bradycardia. It's very, very common in premature babies, though it's sometimes caused by other problems such as low
blood sugar or an infection.'

'Is it—does it mean he's at risk of cot
death?' Sara asked.

'No, that's something totally separate.
Because Liam's premature, the respiratory
centre in his brain—the bit that makes him
breathe—is immature. That means he takes
bursts of great big breaths, followed by very
shallow breaths or the pauses we call apnoea.
The pauses will happen more when he's sleeping, but the good news is that by the time he
gets to the date when he was actually due, his
condition will be a lot better.'

'And he can go home?'

'When we're happy with him, yes,' Claire
said. 'Did Eliot explain the treatment to you?'

'Yes. He spent ages talking to me—he was
so kind. He even gave me a leaflet, but I can't
find it and—'

'It's OK,' Claire said, squeezing her hand.
'There's a lot to take in and it's scary, having
to leave your baby up here when you want him
at home with you. What we're doing at the

moment is something called CPAP—continuous positive airway pressure. What that means is that the little tubes up Liam's nose give him oxygen under pressure. He's also got an apnoea alarm, which will sound if he hasn't taken a breath in a set number of seconds. Don't worry if the alarm goes off a lot—it doesn't necessarily mean that he's not breathing, as there are lots of false alarms. But we set the machine at a fairly low level because it's better to be on the safe side. When the alarm goes off, the nurse will check to see if Liam's breathing. If he isn't, she'll try to stimulate his breathing by rubbing his feet. She might give him some extra oxygen to help him through the sticky patch, and we'll keep a very close eye on him.'

'But he's going to be all right?'

Claire nodded. 'It's really common—and if he responds well, we might be able to let you monitor him at home if that's what you'd like to do. It's early days right now, but he seems to be responding. And you're doing a great job, talking to him and letting him know his mum's here. That's helping a lot.' Claire smiled. 'Don't worry if you can't remember what I've said. Ask any of us, any time, if you're worried. That's what we're here for, and we won't think you're wasting our time.'

'I just feel so stupid,' Sara said.

'Not at all. You're worried about your baby, there's a lot to take in, and we're here to give you all the support you need.' Claire smiled at her again. 'I'll pop in to see you later, when I've finished my ward round.'

Some time later, Eliot leaned against the doorway of Claire's office. 'Coming for some lunch?'

'Sorry. I've got piles and piles of paperwork to do,' Claire hedged.

'Oh, for goodness' sake. It won't kill you to leave it for half an hour,' Tilly said, overhearing the conversation. 'Go and have lunch with your husband.'

Eliot grinned. 'This is our big bad dragon consultant you're talking to. Treat her like ''little wifey'' and we'll be clearing up your charred remains.'

'Listen, you two, some of us have work to do around here,' Claire protested.

'Kiss her into submission. I dare you,' Tilly said with a grin.

To Claire's horror, Eliot did precisely that. He walked into her office, picked her up off her chair and sat her on her desk, then murmured in her ear, 'Everyone's expecting a show. Let's do it.' And then he proceeded to kiss her thoroughly.

A show. He was doing this for show, Claire reminded herself, even as her fingers threaded through his hair. Even as her mouth opened under his. Even as she kissed him back and the fireworks went off in her head again.

Eliot broke the kiss. 'Lunch,' he said. He took her hand and tugged. 'Now.'

Claire slid off her desk and trotted meekly behind him.

Once they'd left the ward, she dropped his hand.

'Sorry about that,' Eliot said, knowing that he was lying. He wasn't sorry in the slightest that he'd kissed her. It had been the flimsiest possible pretext to kiss her, and he shouldn't have done it—but he'd wanted to. He'd wanted her so badly. Still did. 'You said yourself, Tilly's an incurable romantic. She hasn't been married long. She thinks we're madly in love—and she'll guess something's up if we're strictly hands-off at work.' Flimsier and flimsier. Any minute now, she was going to slap his face.

'She'll think that I, as the ward consultant, am being completely professional and concentrating on my job,' Claire corrected.

He gave her his best little-boy grin. The one he hoped might soften her a little. 'Yes, boss.'

'Right. We now have twenty-seven minutes before I have to be back at my desk. I'm behind on two days' worth of paperwork.'

'Delegate,' Eliot said.

'Delegate?'

'Absolutely.'

She gave him a sidelong look. 'In that case, you're cooking dinner tonight.'

He groaned. 'I fell for that one, didn't I?'

'Yeah.'

At least she was smiling, so she couldn't be that angry with him. Besides, he was pretty sure that she'd kissed him back. It hadn't been just an act for Tilly's sake…had it?

All the same, he didn't take any risks that evening, when Claire came home. *Home.* To spend her first night in his house as his wife. Wife in name only, he reminded himself. That was the agreement.

As promised, he cooked dinner. Ryan then insisted on going through his new school reading book with Claire, and meanwhile Eliot pretended to concentrate on the washing-up—though he noticed how patient she was with the little boy, giving him lots of praise and encouraging him to use as much expression as he could in the dialogue.

Stop it, he warned himself. Just stop it. She likes him, she's used to dealing with a child who has Asperger's because her godson has it too, but she didn't promise to step into the role of Ryan's mum. Just because she'd be perfect for it—and you—it doesn't mean it's going to happen. She doesn't want kids of her own, remember?

When Ryan was in bed, Eliot took a glass of wine to Claire, who was working on a laptop at the dining-room table.

'Thanks,' she said, looking surprised.

'It's the least I can do.' He paused. 'About tonight. I'll sleep on the couch.'

'No.'

His eyes widened. Was she…?

'You're way too tall and you'll get backache. So you'll be fit for nothing at work.'

No. She wasn't suggesting anything. She was thinking of the ward first—as any consultant would. He suppressed the dull ache of disappointment. They'd agreed that last night had been a one-off and from today onwards they'd just be friends. Why had he spent the day hoping that she'd go back on her word? Why had he managed to convince himself that that kiss in her office had meant anything to her?

'We're adults. We can share a bed as friends,' Claire said.

Yeah, right. She might be able to—he was going to need a very long cold shower beforehand. 'Sure,' he said, with a brightness he definitely didn't feel. 'I'll leave you in peace. I'll be catching up with the *BMJ* next door if you need anything.' Preferably me. In bed. Now.

Whoa, boy, he told himself, and left the room before he said something stupid.

Concentrating on a professional journal helped. Once he managed to switch his brain towards work, that was. But his mind kept replaying images of Claire. Claire, with her hair loose and spread over his pillow. Claire, her eyes dark with passion. Claire, her figure lush and curvy, her breasts firm and full.

And it wasn't just the way she looked. It was her perfume, the scent of her hair, the way she tasted.

Hell. He had it bad. And it had to stop, right now.

'I'm heading for bed,' Claire said, looking around the door.

Eliot very nearly said 'Good'. But he plastered a smile on his face. 'I'll just finish this article first,' he said.

'Um, which side do you sleep on?' she asked.

Good question. They hadn't exactly slept a lot last night. Or stuck to one particular side. And he wished he hadn't started thinking about that. 'Whatever,' he said, trying to sound cool and casual, though he felt as if he was burning up.

He spent ages in the shower. With the temperature turned right down. And when he walked into the bedroom, clad in an old T-shirt and a pair of boxer shorts, Claire gave him an enquiring gaze.

'I don't have any pyjamas,' he admitted, climbing into bed beside her.

Bad move. He might just as well have told her that he slept in the buff. And the idea of sleeping with Claire, skin to skin, as he had last night... No. Concentrate on something neutral. The muscles of the pharynx and larynx. Upper constrictor, stylopharyngeal, middle constrictor, ioglossus...

'See you in the morning,' she said, turned over and switched off her light.

He followed suit, turning away from her because he couldn't trust his hands not to wander. Couldn't trust himself not to pull her into his arms, and to hell with their agreement. 'Sleep well,' he said. Though he knew he wouldn't.

Although somehow he did fall asleep. Because it was at stupid o'clock in the morning that he woke, wondering why he felt so warm. And then he realised. Claire was cuddled into him, facing him so that one hand rested against his chest and the other was curved round his waist. One of her legs had slid between his. And he had one hand tangled in her hair and the other cupping her bottom.

The temptation was way, way too much for him. The curtains were thin enough for the streetlight outside to show him the outline of her face. He shifted so that he could kiss the tip of her nose. She murmured in her sleep and tipped her head back, as if for a kiss. He couldn't help kissing her. Just once. Just lightly.

She murmured his name and snuggled closer. His control snapped so fast he was surprised the sound didn't wake up the whole street. This time, he kissed her properly. Demanding. Promising.

She was dreaming. Remembering their single-night honeymoon. Eliot's mouth was coaxing a response from hers, and his skin felt so good under her fingers. He tasted good, he felt good, he smelled good, and she wanted him. Wanted him inside her. Wanted him to take her with him to that incredible place where only they existed, past the fireworks and the stars.

'Yes. Oh, yes,' she murmured as he unbuttoned her pyjamas, stroking them away from her skin, teasing her nipples until they were so hard that they hurt. 'Yes,' she said again as his hands slid lower, exploring, tormenting until she was arching up towards him. And, 'Yes,' she sighed as she felt the pressure of his body over hers, the roughness of his thighs between hers. And, 'Yes,' she murmured as he entered her, his body taking it slow and easy, then his pace increasing as his control slipped.

She arched against him, matching him thrust for thrust, taste for taste, touch for touch. This was the one place she could have what she wanted, in her dreams: the man she loved, making love with her.

Except her eyes weren't closed. They were open. She was in an unfamiliar room and an unfamiliar bed, though the light that seeped through the curtains showed her a very familiar outline.

Eliot's.

This wasn't a dream.

She was in his bed—and they really were making love.

This couldn't be happening. *Shouldn't* be happening. They'd promised they'd stick to just friendship. And yet she could feel her climax starting at the soles of her feet, a warm rippling that spread up her body and gathered momentum until it felt as if she were in the middle of a whirlpool. She buried her mouth in his shoulder to stop herself crying his name out loud and she felt his answering shudder as he, too, reached his climax.

He rolled onto his side and drew her into the curve of his body, holding her close.

She was about to tell him that it shouldn't have happened when he stroked her hair. Tangled the ends round his fingers. Pressed a kiss to the top of her head. She didn't want to break the spell so she said nothing, merely let her head rest on his shoulder. And slowly, slowly they drifted back into sleep, locked in each other's arms.

CHAPTER TEN

'GOOD morning, Mrs Slater.'

Claire glanced up. Eliot was propped on his side, watching her. His face gave nothing away, though she noticed that his eyes were particularly green. Her glance slid lower. He hadn't put his T-shirt back on. And she'd bet good money his boxer shorts were wherever they'd thrown them last night. Along with her own pyjamas.

Hell, hell and double hell. What had they done?

'Good morning,' she replied, hoping that her voice wasn't trembling as much as she thought it was.

'I think,' he said softly, 'we need to talk. Don't you?'

'Um…yes.' But she had no idea what to say. 'Last night…it wasn't meant to happen.'

'No.'

'We agreed. A single-night honeymoon.'

'Uh-huh.'

'And...' She was just digging herself a hole, and she knew it. 'What happens now?' she asked.

'What do you want?'

You. I want you waking me up every morning with a kiss. I want to hold your hand at the seaside as Ryan paddles in front of us. I want to build a snowman with you in the middle of winter and have a snowball fight where you literally sweep me off my feet and kiss me until I don't care that I'm lying on a pile of snow and my feet are freezing. I want *you.*

She hoped she hadn't said any of that aloud. 'What do *you* want?' she asked carefully.

'Hmm.' He traced the line of her jaw with his forefinger. 'Answering a question with a question. That's not fair.'

He hadn't answered either. And *that* wasn't fair. And neither was touching her. It made her remember how it had felt last night. The perfection of making love with him. A perfection she couldn't have. She dragged her thoughts back to the present with difficulty. 'We agreed this was a temporary marriage. Between friends.'

'Which it is.'

The words felt like nails being driven into her heart. Even after what they'd shared, it was still going to be a temporary marriage.

'Except…we're not just friends any more, are we?' he asked softly.

'No.' She forced the word through dry lips. 'Last night…wasn't supposed to happen.'

'But it did.'

Still, she couldn't read his face. What did he want?

'And no matter how good our intentions…I think it's going to happen again.' His voice deepened. 'If we continue sharing a bed.'

If. Such a little word. Such a huge step.

'Or we could,' he said slowly, 'call it a bonus.'

'A bonus?'

'A bonus to our friendship.'

So he wanted their love-making to continue? A dull throb of excitement started low in her belly.

'But…' He rubbed his thumb along her lower lip, and she couldn't help responding, tipping her head back and opening her mouth slightly. 'If we do, there's something we need to talk about. We didn't take any precautions last night. Or the night before.'

No. They'd been too carried away.

Now. She should tell him *now*. Her excitement vanished as abruptly as it had started, replaced by a nagging ache of guilt. 'It's all right,' she mumbled.

'You're on the Pill?' he guessed.

'No.'

'It's the safe time of your cycle?'

No. Tell him *now*, she told herself fiercely. Tell him. But she couldn't. What was happening between them—it was still so new, so tender, so fresh. She had no idea how he'd react when she told him the truth. Would he be angry? Hurt? Disgusted?

She couldn't bear the idea of him rejecting her. Not now.

He clearly took her silence as confirming his guess, because he continued, 'Even so, it's still a risk. So unless your self-control is a damn sight better than mine—'

It wasn't. And she knew he knew it.

'I'll make sure you're protected in future.'

Tell him. Tell him he doesn't need to think about condoms. That there's absolutely no chance of you ever having his baby. *Tell him.*

She opened her mouth, but the wrong words came out. 'Thank you.'

*   *   *

There really was a fairy godmother, Eliot thought. And she'd just waved her magic wand. OK, like Cinderella, he knew his time at the ball was limited—in his case, just until the custody issue was resolved. But until then Claire was his wife. In his life, in his heart, and in his bed.

And maybe, just maybe she might fall in love with him. She might not want their marriage to end. She might become his wife for always.

If he rushed her now, he'd ruin everything. He'd already seen the sheer panic in her dark eyes when he'd brought up the subject of making babies. She'd said it was her safe time, and he knew the risks were small, but if it turned out that she *was* pregnant, it wouldn't be the end of the world.

Now that he thought of it, he rather liked the idea. Curled up with Claire, feeling her belly swell over the next few months as their baby grew. Feeling their little girl kick when he placed a hand on Claire's stomach. A sister for Ryan to adore—a sister who'd follow him about and look up to him and maybe help to unlock the little boy's heart. And he'd be there to take his fair share of nappy changes, middle-of-the-night feeds and cuddles and winding...

Hell, he must have it bad, to be gooey-eyed at the prospect of sleep deprivation and baby vomit!

He gave her a sidelong look. 'So, now we've established that... You're on a late this morning. And Ryan won't be awake for another twenty minutes.' His voice dropped to a husky whisper. 'And I can think of a very nice way to start the day...'

For a moment he thought she was going to refuse. That he'd pushed her too far. But then that sultry light gleamed in her eyes, she smiled and she reached up to pull his head down to hers.

Later that afternoon, Eliot finished examining his patient, reassured the parents and headed straight for Claire's office.

'Can you spare a minute?' he asked.

She glanced up and saw the serious look on his face. 'Sure. What's up?'

'I think we've got a case of NEC. Matthew Rogers.'

NEC—necrotising enterocolitis—could be fatal in a newborn. Claire nodded thoughtfully.

Matthew Rogers was ten days old and had been born two months early with a very low birth weight so he fitted the classic profile of babies who developed NEC. 'Symptoms?' she asked.

'Abdominal distension—I know in prem-mies it's often because they don't have much subcutaneous fat and the abdominal wall dis-tends more, but I think it's more than that in this case. I'd say Matthew's at stage one right now. His obs show we've had problems keep-ing his body temperature normal, he's lethargic and he's scared his mum with a few spells of apnoea. He's not feeding as well as he could do, there's more gastric aspirate—' meaning that Matthew was bringing up more milk '—and there was blood in his last stool.'

'What's his colour like? Pale, mottled, any redness around the abdomen?'

'A bit pale. I think we should do the usual tests—stool sample down to the lab for culture, bloods, and an abdominal X-ray to check it's that and not any other sort of intestinal ob-struction,' Eliot continued. NEC could develop very slowly, or it could get a lot worse very quickly and the baby could die within hours. The baby's abdomen became more distended and a bowel obstruction or ileus formed. This stopped the baby passing stools, and then ascites or fluid developed in the stomach and sometimes the bowel perforated—becoming a surgical emergency.

'Have you checked for an anal fissure?' Claire asked. That was one of the more common reasons for blood in the stools.

'Yes, and there isn't one.'

'Let me know when the X-rays are back, and I'll take a look,' Claire said.

The X-rays confirmed Eliot's diagnosis. 'Well spotted,' Claire said, looking at the film with him. 'The gut wall's thicker than usual, there's dilation of the bowel loops here and here, and intramural gas.' She raised an eyebrow. 'Let's go and talk to Mrs Rogers. And then I'll have a word with the surgical team.'

Eliot introduced Claire to Isla Rogers.

'Eliot's picked up that Matthew has a bit of a problem with his tummy,' Claire said gently. 'It's something called necrotising enterocolitis—NEC, for short. It's a scary name, but all it means is that it's an inflammation that causes injury to the bowel.'

'It's very varied,' Eliot added. 'It might affect just the lining or the whole thickness of the bowel, and it affects various lengths of the bowel, too.'

'But why has he got it?' Isla asked.

'We often don't know why individual babies get it,' Claire said. 'But premature babies have a very immature and fragile bowel. They're very sensitive to change in blood flow, or infection.'

'But he was doing so well! He's ten days old now.' Isla's finger was firmly clutched in her tiny son's fist. 'Is it because I'm not feeding him myself?'

Claire winced inwardly at the question. 'It's more common in formula-fed babies, yes, and there's some evidence that breast milk can help protect against NEC, but that *doesn't* make it your fault,' she emphasised. Isla was clearly worried sick about her small son, and the last thing she needed was to be made to feel guilty because she wasn't breast-feeding.

'I did try, and the midwife tried to help me express milk, but I just couldn't do it,' Isla said.

Claire squeezed her free hand. 'Don't blame yourself. As I said, we often don't know why babies get it.'

'So what are you going to do?'

'We need to rest his gut, so we'll give him his feeds through a drip,' Eliot said. 'We'll also keep a check on him with daily X-rays.'

'He'll need antibiotics to stop any further infection development, and he may need a blood transfusion,' Claire said. 'Hopefully, because we've caught the condition in the early stages, he might not need surgery. We'll follow the treatment for the next seven to ten days, but we'll be keeping a very close eye on him—if we're not happy, we'll ask the surgeons to take a look. They'll do keyhole surgery and what they do first is look at the bowel to assess what's happening. If it's just the innermost lining of the bowel that's affected, the body can actually regrow the lining. But if a whole thickness of the bowel dies, we need to remove it—otherwise the contents of the bowel are likely to spill into his stomach, and that's not good.'

'What happens if he needs surgery?' Isla asked.

'Hopefully it won't come to that, but what the surgeon will do is remove the dead piece of bowel and sew the two ends of the bowel back together—it's called anastomosis,' Eliot said. He exchanged a glance with Claire and decided not to mention the alternatives at that stage—or the possible later risks, such as mal-absorption, or even a 'short bowel' where there wasn't enough bowel for the little boy to absorb the nutrients from his food, or further bowel obstruction caused by scar tissue. Right now, Isla Rogers had enough to worry about.

'And is he—is he going to…?' Isla clearly couldn't bear to say the final word out loud.

'He's got a very good chance of getting through this,' Claire said. 'Around eighty to ninety per cent. He might get another attack of NEC, but our surgeons here are very good and I can assure you we'll keep a very close eye on Matthew. I don't take any risks with my babies.' She smiled wryly. 'Or my mums. So if you or your partner have any questions at any time, we're here to help.'

The days passed and Claire felt as if she really was part of a proper family. How easily she'd slipped into taking Ryan to school on the days when she was on a late, or picking him up when she was on an early. Eliot trusted her enough with his son that he'd agreed to do late shifts as well as days, provided that their duties meant one of them could be there for Ryan.

Ryan had blossomed to the point where he was really responding to his 'social use of language' programme at school and beginning to form the fragile early bonds of friendship with his classmates. Claire had persuaded him out of some of his eating routines, encouraging him to try something new from her plate or even cooking something with her that he'd never tried eating before. And although the grocery shopping took her three times as long—because Ryan wanted to know the ins and outs of how different fruit and vegetables were grown, or wanted to tell her about how tin cans were made, or how wheat grew and was made into pasta—it had stopped being the chore she'd hated doing after her shift. And Ryan had started spending more time with her and Eliot, instead of yearning to rush straight to his computer as soon as he got home.

And then there were the nights... Nights when she and Eliot explored each other by touch and taste, nights when their love-making took them to the other side of paradise, nights when she lay awake just for the pleasure of watching him sleeping and smiling in his dreams.

Neither of them used the L word. And as long as they didn't use the L word, she was safe. She could walk away from their temporary marriage with her heart intact and a lifetime's worth of memories, releasing him to find someone who could give him and Ryan everything they needed.

And then the letter arrived.

Eliot passed it over without comment. Claire, realising immediately that he didn't want to talk about it in front of Ryan, scanned it swiftly. The court had appointed someone to come and see them. Reading between the lines, that meant checking them out. Seeing if they were fit parents for Ryan. And Eliot's solicitor recommended that they both co-operate as fully as possible with the court's wishes.

She looked up and saw the terror in Eliot's eyes. The fear that somehow he'd be found wanting, that his precious son would be taken away.

'It's going to be fine,' she said softly. 'Trust me.'

'Yeah.' But his voice was hollow.

*   *   *

'So you've been married...a month?' Kara Beale asked.

'We've known each other for longer than that,' Eliot said.

Kara nodded and made another note. He knew without having to be told what she was writing. That he'd rushed into marriage with the first person he could find after getting the letter from Malandra's solicitors. That it was clearly a fake marriage, a desperate attempt to keep custody of his son.

Claire had warned him. Why, why, *why* hadn't he listened?

Then he became aware that Kara was looking at him expectantly. As if waiting for an answer. He bit his lip. 'I'm sorry. I didn't hear what you said.'

'She was asking how Ryan felt about me.' Claire came into the room and stood behind him, sliding her arms round his shoulders and kissing the top of his head. 'I dunno. Men. They never pay attention, do they?' She kissed him again. 'Sorry I'm late.' She held her hand out to Kara. 'You must be Kara Beale. I'm Claire, and I'm sorry I wasn't here when you arrived. I had intended to take a half-day but I got held up at the ward.'

'Yes, your husband said.'

Yes, and Eliot was sure she hadn't believed a word of it.

Claire sat down next to Eliot. 'Ryan and I get on fine. My godson is the same age as him—he has Asperger's, too, so I already had a good idea of what Ryan's boundaries would be.'

'You're a paediatrician?' Kara asked.

'Neonatal specialist—I work with babies in the special care unit,' Claire confirmed.

'And that's how you met?'

'Yes.'

'And you're Eliot's boss?'

Claire grinned. 'At work, yes. At home, no—isn't that right, oh, lord and master?'

She was *teasing* him? When the woman in front of them had the power to recommend that Ryan be taken away? Eliot's outrage died as he realised what Claire was doing. Showing that they had a normal family relationship, with fun and laughter and silliness as well as taking their shared parenting of Ryan seriously. 'She has bossy tendencies,' Eliot said, teasing her back. 'But I have a picture of her covered with flour after she and Ryan made

biscuits last week. All I have to do is acciden-
tally let it fall out of my locker at work...'

'Horrible man.' Claire pulled a face at him.
'Kara, can I get you a drink of anything?
Coffee, tea, something cold?'

'Something cold would be lovely, please.'

'Juice?' Claire suggested.

'Please.'

'OK. Usual, love?' she asked Eliot.

'Please.'

By the time Claire came back with the
drinks, Eliot had relaxed completely, answering Kara's questions in as much detail as he
could. He even suggested showing Kara
around the house.

'This is Ryan's room,' he said.

Kara raised an eyebrow. 'It's very neat, for
a seven-year-old's bedroom.'

'A seven-year-old with Asperger's,' Claire
corrected. 'Everything has to be in its place.
And if you don't put it in the *right* place, it
really unsettles him.'

'Are these his drawings?' Kara asked, seeing the cardboard file labelled 'Rocket Plans'
on the chest of drawers.

'Yes, but don't expect to see pictures of
people,' Eliot warned. 'He draws maps and

rockets and dinosaurs. Children with Asperger's prefer to deal in facts, not emotions.'

Kara flipped through the file. 'So he's going to be an astronaut?'

'Once he's built the rocket he designed. In between being a palaeontologist, a marine biologist and a vulcanologist,' Eliot said wryly.

'He's got a portfolio career all mapped out,' Claire said with a grin.

Kara nodded and followed them back onto the landing. 'And this is your room?' she asked, looking at the closed door.

Eliot and Claire stared at each other. Panic telegraphed between them, then Eliot nodded. If they didn't let Kara see their room, she'd think they had something to hide. That Claire didn't even live there perhaps.

He opened the door and both he and Claire groaned in horror. In contrast to the rest of the house—which was neat and orderly—their bedroom was messy. Very messy. Claire's hairdryer was still plugged in on the floor in front of the cheval mirror and, worse, the bed was extremely rumpled. Making it obvious that they hadn't just slept in it the previous night.

Claire's face flamed. 'I was on early shift this morning. You were the last one up,' she muttered. 'I thought you said you were going to…'

'I was.' Eliot's face was equally flushed. 'But when we got back from school, I blitzed downstairs. I, um, forgot about our room.'

'Oh, lord. I'm so sorry,' Claire mumbled to Kara. 'Um, we're not usually…'

'It's fine,' Kara said with a smile. 'Like you said—men, eh?'

'Yeah. And, please, tell me you pegged the washing out,' Claire said, looking at Eliot. 'I put the washing machine on before I left this morning.'

Eliot shifted uncomfortably. 'I meant to. But I did the grocery run on the way home from school—'

'And you forgot about the washing,' Claire finished. She rolled her eyes. 'Right. It's a tumble dryer job tonight, then—because Ryan spilled milk over his school trousers yesterday morning so his spare pair was in the wash, too.'

'We're not usually this disorganised,' Eliot said to Kara.

'We were, um, panicking a bit. About your visit,' Claire admitted. 'And now we've proved we're hopeless.'

'You're both working full time and you're fitting your work around your son,' Kara said. 'The judge isn't looking for domestic perfection—just what's right for Ryan.'

'That's all we want, too,' Claire said softly.

'Does Ryan call you Mummy?' Kara asked.

Pain knifed through Claire and she struggled to hide it. She didn't want to jeopardise Eliot's chances of keeping his son. Not now, when they'd worked so hard to prove they were right for him. A normal family. 'He calls me Claire,' she said carefully. 'We're not rushing him into anything. We're taking it at his pace.'

'But you got married fairly quickly,' Kara said.

'We'd known each other for a while,' Claire said. 'And we checked it with Ryan first. He was happy about me moving in here. And we kept the wedding small because he doesn't cope well with large groups. That's also why he doesn't go to the school disco and why he's got one-to-one support at school during playtime.'

Kara nodded. 'Well, I think I've seen enough,' she said. 'I'll be making my report to the court.'

'And you agree that he's better off with us?' Eliot asked.

'I'm sorry, I can't discuss my report with you,' Kara said.

He winced. 'Sorry. I shouldn't have asked. It's just…we don't want to lose him.'

'What about having a family of your own?' Kara asked.

'He *is* our family,' Claire said firmly. 'If you mean, what about more babies—no.'

'So you don't want any more children?'

Claire dug her nails into her palms. She'd guessed this would be one of the questions asked. And she'd prepared her answers—she just hadn't quite prepared enough for the pain. The longing. The wrench. 'It wouldn't be fair to Ryan,' she said softly. 'It'd be a big age gap and we don't want him to feel pushed out.'

'But you're newlyweds,' Kara said.

'And I've recently been made consultant,' Claire said quietly.

'So you have to work longer hours?'

'I've been acting consultant for the past six months,' Claire explained. 'So it's just a change in title—my responsibilities are the same. And Ryan comes first.'

'I see. Well, thank you both. You've been very open and honest,' Kara said.

Honest. If only she knew, Claire thought, but she smiled politely.

When Eliot had seen Kara out, he came back and put his arms round Claire. 'Thank you. You were brilliant,' he said. 'I was panicking until you came in.'

'I'm only sorry I was late.'

'Not your fault.' He swallowed. 'Do you think she believed we were really married?'

'After the washing machine—yes.' Claire didn't dare mention their bedroom.

'Malandra's got a huge house,' Eliot said. 'Probably with a housekeeper. I bet washing would never be a problem in her house. Or mess. And she could give Ryan a proper play-room.'

'But she's not *you*,' Claire reminded him. 'She isn't the one Ryan depends on. And I'm sure a judge will see that. You'll be fine.'

Eliot said nothing, but she could see in his eyes that he didn't believe her. If only she could wave a magic wand and make everything all right. An ideal world, where she'd be

Eliot's wife and Ryan's mother in reality. Where her temporary family would become permanent.

Except she didn't have a magic wand.

And time was running out for her temporary family.

CHAPTER ELEVEN

WAITING. That was the worst thing, Eliot thought. Waiting to find out if Ryan was going to be taken away from him. Waiting to find out if he'd become a weekend-and-holidays father—fitting in as much as he could into the few snatched hours they had together each week. No more bedtime stories. No more sinking submarines in the bath. No more earnest discussions about rockets and the best shape for a rocket's nose and what astronauts ate and how long it would take to get to Mars. Not being the one to nag about homework and listen to his son reading. Not being the one who kissed better a bumped head or a scraped knee. Not being the tooth fairy and writing little letters from her in answer to Ryan's questions about what exactly she was going to do with the teeth and if she could leave her wand behind, please, so Ryan could examine it and see how it worked.

The loss gaped before Eliot like an abyss. A deep, dark, empty and unknown place. He really, really didn't want to go there. And he didn't even have Claire's hand to pull him back—not really. What she'd said to Kara Beale kept echoing through his head. No more children. *It wouldn't be fair to Ryan. It'd be a big age gap and we don't want him to feel pushed out... I've recently been made consultant.*

All excuses. Because Claire didn't want a family with him.

He knew why. She'd married him solely as his friend, to help him keep Ryan. She shared his bed, made love with him every night, but... But. The word was so huge it blocked his throat. *But* she wasn't in love with him. She'd never said a word to him about love.

For the fourth night in a row, he was awake at exactly eight minutes past two. Stark staring awake. Thinking of what was going to happen. Scared he couldn't stop it. And not even the soft regularity of Claire's breathing beside him could stop the terror flowing through him and forcing his eyes open. Because when he lost Ryan, he knew he'd lose her, too.

The only place he could function properly was work. Maybe that was because so many of the parents on the ward were in the same position as he was—scared spitless that they'd lose their children. The only difference was that his son was seven years older than their babies. So instead of being one of them, he was the one they looked to for hope. The one who could keep everything going.

'It doesn't feel right, being here,' Janet Crombie said, cuddling her baby. 'Look at all the little ones around us—they're tiny and my Scott's so…'

Scott was a whopping ten-pounder, despite being born two weeks early. He was large for dates with the chubby, almost cherubic face which was typical of a baby whose mother had had diabetes in pregnancy.

'He's doing fine,' Eliot reassured her.

Janet didn't look reassured. 'When they told me I had gestational diabetes, I read everything I could about it and how it could affect the baby. I was so strict about what I ate, what I drank. I really, really tried hard to keep my blood sugar right for my baby.'

'Which is the best thing you could have done. This isn't your fault, so don't blame yourself,' Eliot said. 'Low blood sugar is very common just after birth, particularly in premature babies. The baby's blood sugar is his main source of energy in the first two hours of his life, and the levels of glycogen or stored sugar in his liver fall at the same time.'

'So it's nothing to do with my diabetes?' Janet asked.

'Babies of mums who had gestational diabetes are more likely to have low blood sugar as newborns,' Eliot admitted. 'That's why we're screening him. We're testing him regularly to check his blood sugar—that's just one drop of blood on a chemical strip. We've got a catheter in his umbilical artery so taking a blood sample won't hurt him at all,' he explained.

'So what happens if his blood sugar stays too low?' Janet asked.

'Because you kept your diabetes under good control,' Eliot said, 'we should find that his body corrects the levels itself. By the time he's twelve hours old, as long as he's feeding well, he's highly unlikely to have any more problems.'

'What if he does?' Janet asked.

'We'll see other signs—he'll look pale and sweaty, and his heart rate will speed up,' Eliot said. 'We'll get you to feed him more frequently and keep an eye on his blood sugar. If it's still too low we'll give him sugar water by a drip, as well as getting you to feed him frequently.'

'So he's not going to get brain damage or anything?'

Clearly Janet had read up on the possible effects on the baby as well as on herself. 'We're keeping a close eye on him, so it's highly unlikely,' Eliot reassured her. 'Once he's feeding normally, he'll be absolutely fine. And he's not going to have blood sugar problems in later life either.'

Janet drooped visibly, and he patted her shoulder. 'Hey. You'll both be fine.'

'I— Well, I was just worried about him,' Janet said.

'Of course you were. You're his mum.'

'And I feel such a fraud. All the other mums in here have these little tiny, delicate babies and half of them are too small or too ill to be cuddled, and here's Scott so huge and...' She broke off on a sob.

'Hey.' Eliot handed her a tissue. 'We're here to help babies who need us, whether they're big or small, early or late. You're here because we want to keep an eye on Scott. And as soon as we're happy with him—which, all being well, should be later tonight—you can both go back down to the maternity ward.'

'Thanks. I'm just being silly,' Janet said.

'Not at all.' Eliot gave her a wry smile. 'I've got a seven-year-old. And I'm just the same about him as you are about Scott.' Though how much longer Ryan could stay with him… He pushed the thought away and forced himself to continue smiling. 'I'll be back to check on him shortly. If you're worried about anything in the meantime, just ask.'

The shadows under Eliot's eyes deepened as the date for the custody hearing drew closer. Claire tried to soothe him as best she could, holding him close at night and showing him with her body how much she loved him, telling him without words that she was there for him.

She almost told him she loved him. But she couldn't put that much pressure on him. She had to keep it to herself how worried she was, too, worried that he'd lose his son. Worried that Ryan would suffer. Worried that if they lost the custody battle, Eliot would yearn for another baby to help fill the hole in their lives, a baby she couldn't give him.

And worried that if she told him she loved him, the whole fragile house of cards they'd built together would all come tumbling down.

At last it was the morning of the hearing.

Eliot and Claire both took Ryan to school, and Eliot hugged his son as if he'd never see him again. As if his heart was breaking.

'Dad,' Ryan said, wriggling away.

'Sorry, son. Just— I love you. Have a good day,' Eliot said. 'Ally's picking you up to-night. You're going to have tea with Jed.'

'Cool,' Ryan said. He gave Claire a hug. 'Bye,' he said, and walked off through the school doors.

'Come on,' Claire said softly. 'I'll drive.'

'No, it's OK. I'll do it. I'm fine,' Eliot said.

She heard the slight wobble in his voice. 'Everything's going to be all right. Trust me,' she said, squeezing his hand.

They met their solicitor outside the court, then sat with him until their case was called.

It was the first time Claire had ever seen Malandra. Eliot didn't even have a photograph of her in the house, and he'd told her once that he'd given all the wedding photographs to Malandra via her parents. Her resemblance to

Ryan was striking—the same mid-brown hair, the same stunning cornflower-blue eyes, the same shaped face. Despite the careful make-up, she looked as strained as Eliot did. Clearly she wanted her son back.

As for the husband, he looked the typical business type, soberly dressed in a dark suit with a white shirt and an understated tie. No hint of anything flashy, just concern for his wife. Claire tried to imagine him as stepfather to Ryan—and couldn't.

What sort of life would Ryan have with them? Would they understand his little rituals, his little routines? Would they encourage him to follow his interests?

But it wasn't her place to make judgements or demands. When it came down to it, Ryan wasn't her son. He was Malandra's. And this was between Eliot and Malandra.

Kara Beale gave her report to the judge. Ryan was growing up in a stable home, with two parents who clearly adored him and knew enough about his condition to make his life as easy as possible.

But… Ryan's birth mother had had a difficult time. She'd had postnatal depression, which had caused her to walk out on her son.

She'd undergone a very long course of treatment, and now she was fine. Remarried. In a stable relationship, and they could give Ryan everything he needed. They understood that Ryan needed careful handling but were prepared to do everything they could. Malandra had read up on Asperger's and was a member of a support group for parents whose children had the condition. Although she wasn't medically qualified, she was bright and perfectly able to understand the medical implications of Ryan's condition.

Claire glanced at Eliot. His face was grey. Hell. They sounded so evenly matched... If the judge ruled in Malandra's favour, Eliot would never recover. But the judge couldn't do that. He couldn't possibly. Please, she willed, please rule in Eliot's favour.

It was Eliot's turn to take the stand. She squeezed his hand. 'You'll be fine,' she said softly. 'Just tell the truth.'

Tell the truth.

So Eliot did. 'I love my son,' he said. 'I've cared for him single-handedly for the past five years. And, yes, I know now that Malanda had severe postnatal depression. At the time I didn't realise how bad things were for her. I tried my best to sort things out between the two of us after she left. But it's just been Ryan and me for all those years. He's only seven, and he has special needs.' A muscle twitched in his jaw. 'If he goes to live with his mother, he's going to have to accept huge changes in his life—a new home, a new school, new doctors and only having limited access to me, the person he's relied on all his life. Any small child would have difficulty coping with changes like that, but for a child with Asperger's they're so much bigger.' His knuckles were white as he gripped the edge of the table. 'I worry that he's not going to cope. I worry that this is going to be too much for him. And I don't want to lose my son.' He took a deep breath. 'I'm happy to let Malandra and her husband have access, though they'll need to take things slowly and carefully, go at Ryan's pace. And...' He spread his hands. 'Please, don't take my son away from me. That's all I have to say.'

'You've remarried very recently,' Malandra's solicitor said. 'In fact—not long after my client applied for custody. One might question the validity of the marriage.'

'It's perfectly legal,' Eliot said.

'And very convenient,' the solicitor said.

Eliot smiled thinly. 'It might look that way, but I can assure you it isn't.' Well, the odds were that he was going to lose them both anyway. He had nothing else left to lose. And Claire herself had urged him to tell the truth, hadn't she?

'I fell in love with Claire months ago—the first time I ever saw her. I don't know what it was—the way she smiled, the colour of her eyes, her perfume. There was just something about her, something that drew me. And the more I got to know her at work, the more I fell in love with her. She's clever, kind and beautiful. She's funny. She makes me laugh. She's a fabulous doctor. And she's changed my life—she's brought sunshine into it. For Ryan, too. She understands him and he adores her. He hardly ever mentions people—teachers, friends at school and the like—but the day he met her, he recognised how special she was and wouldn't stop talking about her after that.' He glanced over towards her, then back at the solicitor. 'Since Claire's been in my life, my house has actually become my home instead of just the place where I live. Because I know she's there with me.'

Tell the truth.

And yet Claire knew Eliot was lying.

He'd never said he loved her. Ever. Not on their wedding night when they'd first made love, or on the nights since. He'd never, ever told her that he loved her.

So why was he saying it to the court instead of to her? Why would he tell complete strangers and his ex-wife before he told Claire herself?

And then a seriously nasty thought hit her. Was he only saying it because he thought it was what they wanted to hear?

Ice trickled down her spine. She could remember someone else swearing he loved her. Loved her and only her. Would be faithful to their dying day. The same person who'd already broken his pledge to 'love and honour until death us do part'—and broken that pledge countless times. The same person who'd taken away her right to choose her future.

She'd promised herself she wouldn't fall for the same trick twice. And now here she was, listening to Eliot Slater declare his love for her in front of total strangers and his ex-wife. A love he'd never once admitted to her.

Give him a chance, her heart said. You agreed to be friends. And you never told him that you loved him either. Maybe he was holding back because he was scared you didn't feel the same and would leave him.

Yeah, right, her common sense said. This is the man who reminded you, the day after our wedding night, that our marriage was temporary. He's saying he loves you because he thinks it's what people want to hear. Just like Paddy. Oiling the wheels, making everything smooth, making people happy.

He's not like Paddy, her heart protested.

And you only want to think that because you don't want to face the truth, her common sense sneered. That he and Ryan aren't your real family and never could be. That's Ryan's mother sitting over there. Not you. Eliot likes you and the sex is good, but that's where it stops. He doesn't really love you—or he would have told you before today.

Claire folded her hands in her lap and dug her nails in her palm to stop herself howling aloud. And if she looked miserable, she hoped people would think it was worry at the prospect they'd lose Ryan.

She barely heard Malandra's tearful deposition that she'd lost five years of her son's life and didn't want to lose any more. She barely heeded the independent specialist's report about Asperger's and the particular difficulties of children with the condition in adjusting to change. She didn't register the judge summing up, until Eliot was hugging her, squeezing the life out of her.

'I can't believe it,' he choked.

Her face was wet and it took her a while to realise that Eliot was crying, not her. She felt as if she were bleeding inside. All that, and they'd lost Ryan.

'He's ours, Claire. He's still *ours*.'

So this was it. The beginning of the end. They'd stay together for a few more months to make it look good. And then…nothing.

She couldn't bear it. She couldn't bear the long drawn-out pain of knowing that every day from now on was closer to the time she'd be out of their lives for ever. Eliot's temporary wife, Ryan's temporary mother.

If Eliot hadn't lied in court, she could have handled it. But he'd said it. He'd said the L word. And she needed out of this marriage.

She was crying, and she knew he thought they were tears of joy, that all the worry they'd had about Ryan was over. But these tears ate into her soul like acid. She couldn't go on living a lie.

Later that evening, when Ryan was in bed, Eliot cracked open a bottle of champagne.

'Not for me, thanks,' Claire said as he began to fill a glass.

There was something brittle in the quality of her voice that alerted him. That, and the memory that they'd shared a bottle of champagne on their wedding night.

He frowned. 'Claire? Is something wrong?'

'We agreed on a temporary marriage,' she said. 'And now it's assured that you have custody, there's no reason for us to stay married.'

But… He loved her. He'd said it out loud, in a court of law. He'd told the truth. He loved her.

And then it hit him. Really hit him. She'd meant it all along. The temporary bit. She didn't love him. And no matter how much he loved her, it wouldn't be enough for both of them.

'There's something I ought to tell you.'

She looked nervous. She was twisting the ring on her finger—the wedding ring they'd chosen together—and her eyes were almost black, her pupils were so huge.

Eliot's heart speeded up. What was she going to tell him? That there was someone else— she'd fallen in love with someone else?

At least she was going to tell him face to face. Unlike Malandra. At least she wasn't just going to walk out of his life and leave him a note to find among the ruins of his life.

He forced himself to stay calmer than he felt. 'What's that?'

'I, um, had chlamydia a few years back.'

Chlamydia. He struggled to take it in. Claire had had a sexually transmitted disease?

'I wasn't aware of it at the time. I had no symptoms.'

There were no symptoms in up to seventy per cent of cases. Eliot knew that.

'I had no unusual discharge, no stinging feeling during urination, no bleeding outside the norm in my menstrual cycle, no pain during sex.'

She was telling him in medical terms. Coldly, calmly, clinically.

'The first time I realised something was wrong was when I had pain in my lower abdomen. Low, dragging, cramping pain. I saw my GP. She suggested I have a test. A test at the…' Claire swallowed hard '…local sexual health clinic. And I found out that I had chlamydia. I'd had it for so long that it had developed complications. Pelvic inflammatory disease.'

The world seemed to tilt and sway on its axis. And certain things became horribly clear. He tried to open his mouth, tried to say something, but his voice simply refused to work. All he could do was listen.

'A course of antibiotics cleared the chlamydia—for my husband, too.'

Her husband. The one who'd had the affair… Or had *Claire* been the one to have the affair? Had she caught chlamydia from sleeping around? Was that why she'd been so upset about Estée Harrold, the woman who'd had an affair resulting in a baby with rhesus haemolytic disease—because she'd done exactly the same thing and got caught out?

'I was clear at the six-month check. But I had laparoscopic investigations. It turned out that my Fallopian tubes were so badly scarred and blocked I can't ever have children.'

So her 'I don't want children' stance had all been a lie. She'd wanted them all right—but she couldn't have them. So he and Ryan had been perfect for her, a ready-made family.

Their whole marriage had been based on a lie.

And he'd stupidly told her he loved her. In public. In front of the whole world. How she must have laughed at him inside. Because she hadn't wanted him. She'd only really wanted his son.

'I think it would be best,' Claire said quietly, 'if I packed my things and left tonight.'

She wanted out. Well, fine. He couldn't handle another relationship based on a lie. On thinking that the woman he loved actually might love him back, when all along she didn't. Or at least didn't love him enough, didn't love him for himself. 'Yes,' he said hoarsely.

'Tell...' Her voice cracked. 'Tell Ryan that I've had to go away to work. Tell him it's not his fault. Tell him I love him.'

'Yes.' He couldn't force any more words out. Didn't want to sink even lower, beg her to stay and learn to love him, learn to want him as much as she wanted a child of her own.

It didn't take her long to pack. And when the door closed behind her as she walked out of his life, Eliot took the still full bottle of champagne and threw it at full force onto the stone flags of his kitchen floor, watching the glass splinter into as many pieces as his heart.

CHAPTER TWELVE

'ALLY, it's me.'

'What's up? Is Ryan all right?' Ally asked.

'Yeah. I just wondered if I could stay the night.' Claire kept her voice calm. Just.

'What's happened?'

'I told you before. We got married so Eliot could keep Ryan. You know he won custody today. So our temporary marriage is now over.'

'Where are you?'

'In the car. Sitting outside your house, actually,' Claire said, gripping her mobile phone tightly.

The phone went dead. Ally's front door opened and she simply held out her arms. Claire stumbled out of the car towards her best friend, and finally allowed her tears to fall.

'Take a sickie,' Ally said, the next morning.

Claire shook her head. 'I'll be fine.'

'Yeah, right. Your eyes are so swollen you can hardly see. I bet you didn't sleep for more than three minutes at a stretch last night, and you're in no fit state to concentrate. Think of your patients. Take a sickie.'

'I've got to face Eliot at some point. And I knew the score all along,' Claire protested.

'And you convinced yourself that it wasn't going to end that way.' Ally sighed. 'I can't believe you never told me about the chlamydia either.'

'I felt too dirty,' Claire said simply.

'But it wasn't your fault! It was Paddy's! Ooh, I could...' Ally growled. 'Just as well he's in Ireland or I'd be kicking his backside for him. In fact, I—'

'Just leave it, Ally.'

The deadness in her voice made Ally pause in mid-rant. She hugged her friend. 'OK. I'm sorry. But I'd still like to punch his lights out on your behalf. And Eliot's, come to think of it.'

'It isn't *his* fault. He was upfront about the situation. You even told me not to do it,' Claire reminded her.

'Yeah. And I'm not going to say, ''I told you so.'' I just wish things were different.'

'Me, too.' Claire attempted a smile, and failed dismally.

'Take a sickie,' Ally urged again. 'I'll ring in and say you have a migraine.'

'I've never had a migraine in my life!'

'Doesn't mean you can't ever have one,' Ally said. 'Now. Eat that toast, or I'll let Jed create a topping for you.'

The last one had been Marmite and lemon curd. And completely inedible. Despite herself, Claire smiled and forced down half a slice of toast.

'Better,' Ally said. 'And you're taking a sickie as of now. Right?'

'Right,' Claire agreed.

A day's breathing space. A day when she didn't have to see Eliot, long for him and know he was for ever out of reach.

But the next morning Claire knew she had to face him. She borrowed Ally's make-up— luckily they had similar colouring—and put on enough war-paint to hide the dark smudges under her eyes and make herself look much cooler and calmer than she felt. And then she drove to work.

Eliot, of course, was the first person she saw when she walked onto the ward.

'Morning,' she said, lifting her chin.

'Morning.' He didn't meet her gaze.

Just as she'd thought. Now she'd told him about the chlamydia, he despised her. Despised her absolutely.

How had it come to this? They'd been friends before. Good friends. Laughed and joked and teased and enjoyed the same things. The cinema with Ryan. Pizza and garlic bread in his kitchen. Lemon drizzle cake in hers. The dinosaurs at the Natural History Museum. A game of ball in the park. Board games with Ryan to teach him about taking turns and sharing.

Then they'd become lovers. Oh, God. She couldn't handle remembering that. The feel of Eliot's skin against hers, his body heat, his scent, his taste.

And now…nothing.

They managed to remain civil to each other during their shift, but Claire was aware that the hospital grapevine was buzzing. Everyone was talking about them, wondering why they'd split up—because it was only too obvious that they *had* split up. Yet no one was brave enough to ask, even Tilly, and Claire wasn't in the mood for making any public statements.

Later that afternoon, she had busied herself in paperwork when she heard the words she was dreading. And the voice she was dreading. 'Do you have a moment, please, Ms Thurman?'

So cool and formal. Well, she could do the same. 'Of course, Dr Slater.'

Good morning, Mrs Slater. Trust her treacherous heart to remember that. And echo it in the precise intonation Eliot had used.

She stiffened her spine. That was then. This was now. She was at work and she was a professional. Claire Thurman, neonatal consultant. 'What's up?'

'Jessie Hinds. She should need less help breathing now, but she needs more oxygen. Her breathing's difficult, her heart rate's up and I thought I heard a murmur.'

'PDA?' she queried. A PDA or patent ductus arteriosus was very common in premature newborns. Jessie was a thirty-four-weeker who'd come onto the ward the previous day. The day when she'd taken a sickie, Claire thought guiltily. The day when she should have picked it up. 'OK. I'll take over.'

He looked as if he was going to say something, then clearly thought better of it and simply left her office. Well, fine. She didn't want to work with him, and he didn't want to work with her. They could manage perfectly well without each other.

She went in to see Jessie and examined her. Just as Eliot had said, there was a heart murmur. Very faint, but still there.

'What is it?' Rita Hinds asked. 'Dr Slater said something about a blood-vessel problem.'

One day, Claire would stop hurting when she heard his name. One day. She forced herself to concentrate. 'I'm going to need to give Jessie an echocardiogram to make sure, but I think Dr Slater's right and Jessie has a PDA. That's a patent ductus arteriosus,' Claire explained. She drew a swift diagram to help show Rita what was happening. 'The ductus arteriosus is the blood vessel which connects the aorta—that's the main blood vessel of the body, here—to the pulmonary artery, or main blood vessel of the lungs. The ''patent'' bit means that the blood vessel is open.'

'Is it serious?' Rita asked, her eyes widening in horror.

'It's fixable,' Claire reassured her. 'And it's very common in babies who've arrived a bit early—it's not considered a heart malfunction because sometimes it fixes itself as the baby gets older. But first I want to do the echo. It's a sound-wave picture of the heart—a bit like the ultrasound you had when you were pregnant, to show how Jessie was developing—and it will show me the blood flow through the blood vessel I was telling you about, the ductus arteriosus.'

She set up the machine. As soon as the picture formed, she nodded. 'See here? This shows me that the blood vessel is open and blood's flowing through it. So, yes, Jessie has a PDA.' She gently stroked the baby's hand. 'And we're going to sort it out and make you feel much more comfortable, sweetheart.'

'How does it happen?' Rita asked.

'Before birth, the baby gets oxygen through the mum's placenta, so the baby doesn't need to use her lungs. That means very little blood needs to go to the lungs to make them grow. The ductus arteriosus lets the blood bypass the lungs and go to the rest of the body. After the birth, the baby uses her lungs so blood has to go from the pulmonary artery to the lungs to pick up oxygen. In most babies, the ductus arteriosus narrows to let that happen.'

'And in Jess's case?'

'It's stayed open. That means that the lungs are getting too much blood flowing to them. That makes the fluid in the lungs increase, so it's hard for the baby to breathe. And the breathing difficulties make the baby's heart work harder.'

'So she could die?'

'If we don't treat her and it doesn't close on its own, it could cause heart failure,' Claire told her. 'But we're going to treat her and she'll be fine. What I'm going to do is give her a drug which will make the ductus arteriosus narrow and close. She might need a second course of drugs, and if they don't work we have a brilliant surgeon here who can tie off the vessel and make sure Jess is fine.' She smiled. 'And the good news is, it doesn't come back in later life.'

Eliot watched her on the ward. His wife. His beautiful, clever, funny wife, caring for her patients and kind to their parents. It hurt even to look at her. Even to breathe when she was around—to breathe and know with every heartbeat that she'd lied to him. She'd said that she was his friend. Offered to do him a favour. And all the time he'd been the one doing her a favour, providing her with the family she couldn't have.

It hurt. And Ryan hurt, too. The little boy hadn't said anything—it wasn't his way—but Eliot had noticed his son's immediate withdrawal back into his old ways. Two days, Claire had been out of their lives. Two days. And Ryan had gone straight back to insisting on using a certain bowl, a certain spoon, a certain cup. Everything in its place, everything in order. Making sense of the world in the only way he knew how.

Right now, Eliot's world didn't make a lot of sense either. He'd changed the sheets, but still he could smell Claire's perfume in his bed. Or maybe it was just haunting him because he could smell it in his car, on the ward, even in the hospital canteen. And the bed itself felt far too big. He kept waking in the night, feeling cold, wondering why Claire had got up—and then reality slammed back in and he lost her all over again.

Why hadn't she trusted him? If she'd told him right at the start... It would have made a difference. She'd clearly learned from her mistakes or she wouldn't have been so upset by Estée Harrold. And now he thought about it, he understood why she'd been in tears over little Robbie Knights, why it had thrown her so badly—she'd seen a reflection of her own situation. Mandy Knights had had chlamydia and had needed IVF to have a baby of her own. And Claire was in exactly the same position.

If only she'd trusted him. If only she'd loved him the way he'd loved her.

But this wasn't going to work. Grimly, he sat and wrote his resignation letter, citing family matters as his reasons for leaving. Tomorrow he'd find himself a new job. A new post. In another hospital. It meant that he'd have to ask Mrs Forrest to have Ryan for longer after school and probably take him to school as well, but they'd cope. After a fashion.

At least he wouldn't have to face Claire any more. See her and want her and know he couldn't have her. It would be the best thing for all of them. Sensible. He knew all that.

So why did it hurt so much?

'Resigned. I see.' Claire strove to keep her voice even. She hadn't expected this—that he'd remove himself entirely from her life. But who had she been trying to kid? He didn't want her anyway. Better not to see him than to have to face him every day and wish things were different. Better not to have a strained atmosphere on the ward. Better not to...

'I'll ring Kelly and see if she wants to come back early.' Or even at all. 'In the meantime, can you organise me some cover, please, Jane?'

'Will do,' the human resources officer said.

'Thanks.' Claire replaced the receiver. Well, that was it. All over, bar writing him a reference for his next post. And Eliot was a good doctor. The fact that he'd rejected her so harshly had nothing to do with his medical skills, the way he dealt with the patients and the parents and the other staff. It was personal.

Had been, she corrected herself. Because they wouldn't see each other ever again.

The fact that she hadn't even been able to say goodbye to Ryan... Well, it was for the best. A scene would only have upset the little boy. But she couldn't help wondering how he was, if he was all right, if Eliot had told him about Malandra and was starting to help him form bonds with his real mother. The mother Claire could never be.

Stop it, she told herself, and opened the data file for her research project. This was a closed episode in her life. From now on she was sticking to her career. Working until she made senior consultant, then professor. It was what she'd planned before she'd met Eliot. Nothing had changed. And with every breath she took, the pain got worse.

'You're working too hard,' Tilly said, a week later.

'I'm fine,' Claire said.

'No, you're not.' Tilly closed the door behind her and sat on Claire's desk. 'What happened?'

'Thanks for your concern, but I don't want to talk about it.'

Tilly sighed. 'I'm not going to spread it as gossip.'

'I know, Tills.' Claire gave a poor attempt at a smile. 'But it's in the past, and nothing's going to change the situation, so it's pointless talking about it.'

'You'll make yourself ill if you carry on like this.'

'Of course I won't.'

'Ally's worried about you, too,' Tilly pointed out.

Claire shrugged. 'I'm fine.' She'd stayed at Ally's until the previous weekend—when it turned out that her tenant wanted to move in with her boyfriend but hadn't been able to find anyone to sublet the house to. Claire had suggested herself—and when she'd moved back in, she'd immediately started decorating. Changing everything round. Obliterating every single memory of Eliot and Ryan in her house. Taking Bess for long runs in between, runs that exhausted the dog as well as her and earned her a ticking-off from Vi—who at least had had the kindness not to pry.

'You're not fine, Claire. But I'm here if you need me,' Tilly said softly.

'I appreciate that. But I'm fine,' Claire insisted.

And she'd nearly convinced herself that she was. Until her office drawer stuck. And when she pulled it out to find out what the problem was, she found Ryan's card to her—the card with the iguanadon. Tears choked in the back of her throat. And then she saw a strip of pictures from a photograph booth. A silly set she and Eliot and Ryan had had taken one afternoon, the three of them crowding the booth, Ryan sitting on their laps. He hadn't been smiling—he never really did smile—but he'd looked happy.

He'd *been* happy. They all had.

And now... Claire crumpled the strip of photographs. There was no point in keeping them. Why torture herself with something she could never have? She threw it at the bin, hard, and it missed. She picked it up again: mistake. Because she couldn't quite let it go. She smoothed the creases out and looked at the pictures again. Stroked Ryan's little face and yearned for the feel of the little boy sitting next to her, chattering excitedly about space and rockets. Touched Eliot's face and yearned for the feel of his arms around her, the feel of his skin against hers.

'It's over, Claire. Forget them,' she told herself out loud.

But she couldn't. And every minute that passed without them seemed to drag on and on and on.

Tomorrow and tomorrow and tomorrow, creeps on this petty pace from day to day... The words echoed in her head. Ally, who'd studied English, had been fond of quoting

Shakespearean soliloquies when they were students. At the time, Claire had thought them a bit over the top. Now she was beginning to understand this one. Tomorrow and tomorrow and tomorrow, stretching out endlessly without Eliot. Without Ryan. Without the family she'd longed for.

How could she bear it?

The only way was to spend more time at work. More time talking to parents, looking after patients, working on her research. Time when she was forced to concentrate on something other than Eliot. Keep herself so busy that she didn't have time to think, so that at night she'd be too tired to do anything other than fall into bed and sleep, too exhausted to dream or remember or think about what might have been.

Two weeks. He'd been working here for two weeks and he still didn't feel as if he fitted in. It wasn't the team's fault—it was because he was still missing Ludbury General, Tilly and Dee and…

No. He had to stop thinking about Claire. For his sanity's sake. He forced himself to concentrate on the parents of the little girl in front of him.

'Beth has something called retinopathy of prematurity—ROP for short. What it means is that the blood vessels in her eyes aren't growing properly.'

'But she's four weeks old now. Why has it taken so long to pick it up?' Lyn asked, her eyes narrowing. 'Why didn't the doctor tell us before?'

'She was born twelve weeks early, and it can develop any time between the time of her birth and when you would have been thirty-two to thirty-four weeks pregnant—that's now.'

'So why aren't her eyes developing properly?' Lyn asked.

Eliot drew a quick sketch. 'In the womb, the blood vessels grow out from the central back of the eye towards the edges—that's here to here—but if the baby's born prematurely there hasn't been enough time for the vessels to grow completely. That's why we get an ophthalmologist—an eye specialist—in to check how the vessels are growing and when they've reached the edges of the eyes. He puts some drops in to dilate the baby's pupils—it doesn't hurt at all—and then he can look through an ophthalmoscope. If the blood vessels are growing normally, that's fine; if it branches abnormally, it's ROP. Which is a lot easier to say than retrolental fibroplasias, the old name for the condition.'

'Does it happen to all premature babies?'

'It's more common in those who are twelve weeks or more too early,' Eliot said. 'If the baby needs more than a certain level of oxygen, she's more at risk. That's why we've been monitoring what we call the partial pressure of oxygen in Beth's blood, through four-hourly blood samples and the pulse oximeter here.'

'Is she going to go blind?'

'Hopefully not,' Eliot said. 'There are three stages of ROP, and Beth's at stage two. In the first two stages, it can clear up on its own. At stage one, you see a line at the edge of the blood vessels...' He drew another diagram to show Lyn what he was talking about. 'And at stage two it becomes a ridge. If it develops to stage three, the eye specialist will need to treat it to stop the abnormal blood vessels detaching the retina from the outer lining of the eye. What he'll do is treat the inner lining of the eye at the end of the abnormal blood vessels to stop them growing any more. The treatment sounds frightening, but it will lessen the chances of Beth going blind. She's more likely to need glasses in early childhood, or have a lazy eye or a wandering eye, so she'll need to have very regular eye check-ups.'

'But she's going to be all right?'

'We'll do our best,' Eliot said, smiling reassuringly.

Though his smile felt fake and his heart felt hollow. Locuming at the hospital in Birmingham had seemed a good idea at the time. Away from Ludbury, away from Claire. But driving to work gave him too long on his own, too much time to think. Too much time to miss Claire and wonder if he'd done the right thing. To wonder whether living a lie and at least having her near him would have been better than living in this lonely, miserable, *empty* space without her.

But it was too late.

CHAPTER THIRTEEN

'RYAN? I've called you three times, son. Teatime!' Eliot said, calling up the stairs.

Still no response. He sighed. Ryan was sulking big time. But it was hardly surprising. Yesterday had been difficult—more than difficult—when Ryan had met his birth mother for the first time in more than five years. Despite Eliot's warnings, Malandra had tried to take things too far, too fast. Tried to hug him before he was ready. Tried to get him to smile and laugh and do all the things that other seven-year-old boys might do. But Ryan had rejected her outright and had been withdrawn and silent ever since, even with his father.

Eliot put his head round the door to Ryan's room and his heart contracted painfully. Ryan wasn't there. The computer was still on—still making the noises he'd assumed meant that Ryan was playing his favourite game, the maths one with the pirate rats—but Ryan was nowhere to be seen.

'Ryan? Ryan?' Eliot went from room to room. There was still no sign of his son. Ryan wasn't hiding in a wardrobe or in his 'den' behind the sofa. Not in the bathroom, not behind a door, not in the garden—the back door was locked and anyway he would have had to go past Eliot to get to it.

So where was he? *Where was he?*

'Think. Stop panicking. Think,' he told himself out loud. 'There's a logical answer. Ryan's logical. There'll be a pattern to follow.'

Last time Ryan had disappeared, he'd gone to Ludbury General. But that had been to find his father—and Eliot was in the house. Unless…

Claire. Ryan had told Malandra that she wasn't his proper mummy and he wanted Claire. He must have gone to find Claire.

Eliot checked his wallet. He wasn't sure if he was more worried or relieved to find it empty. Ryan must have taken the money and he knew the way to the hospital—number 17 bus, four stops. Change to a number 20 bus to the hospital. Fourth floor.

He couldn't have been gone for long enough to reach Ludbury General, so there was no point in ringing the ward to see if Ryan was

258 THE REGISTRAR'S CONVENIENT WIFE

there. He was probably on a bus right now so Eliot would meet him there. Keep him safe.

He broke all the speed limits on the way to the hospital. Parked the car and didn't bother to get a ticket—he didn't want to waste any time. Headed for Reception.

'Have you seen a little boy, please? About so high...' He indicated Ryan's approximate height. 'Blue eyes, brown hair, wearing jeans and a navy blue T-shirt with a T-Rex dinosaur on it?'

The receptionist shook her head. 'Sorry.'

'OK.' So either he hadn't arrived or he was already at the ward. Eliot glanced at his watch. He had no idea when Ryan had left, so there was only one thing for it.

He had to face Claire.

He didn't wait for the lift, knowing how slow it could be. He took the stairs three at a time. Please, please let Ryan be there. Please, let him be with her. Please.

He tapped in the security code at the door to the ward, then strode down to Claire's office. The door was closed, which meant she was probably in a meeting. He felt a flash of guilt at interrupting, but Ryan had to come first. He had to find Ryan. He knocked on the door and barely waited for her to call 'Come in' before he was inside her office.

Her face bleached with shock as she saw him. 'Eliot.'

She looked like hell, he registered. Like he felt. But right now wasn't about them. It was about his son. 'Is Ryan here?'

'Ryan? No.'

'He *must* be.'

'Eliot, I've got no reason to lie to you.'

Not any more. 'He has to be here. I was so sure...' His voice cracked.

The colour that had come back into her face drained away again. 'Are you telling me he's run away?'

'No. Yes.' He raked a hand through his hair. 'I don't know. He's disappeared. I should have known this would happen. I should have—'

'Whoa. Calm down, tell me what happened and we'll work out where he might have gone.'

We. Eliot's lips curved bitterly. They weren't a 'we' any more. 'He's not your problem.'

Claire gave him a withering look. 'This is about finding Ryan, not about you and me. What happened?'

'He spent some time with Malandra yesterday. Apparently it didn't go well—he said she wasn't his mummy and he wanted you. She was pretty upset about it, and what she said didn't make a lot of sense. Ryan refused to discuss it at all—just glued himself to his model-making.' Which was the equivalent of sticking his fingers in his ears and saying, *La, la, can't hear you.*

'I took the day off today in case things were rough at school. He was fine. I brought him home and let him play on the computer while I sorted dinner, but he didn't come when I called him. The computer was still on and making noises as if he was in his pirate program, but he wasn't there. He wasn't anywhere in the house. My wallet was empty.'

'And you thought maybe he'd come here—like he did when he was upset with Fran.'

Eliot nodded, relieved that she'd picked up on his thoughts so quickly. Then again, Claire always had. Claire had been so in tune with him that being without her felt…discordant. Odd. As if he was singing a flat harmony and the main tune had disappeared.

'I haven't seen him, Eliot. And I wouldn't lie to you about that.'

'So where is he, Claire? He could be— Oh, God.' Eliot's breath caught. 'He could be any-where. Lying in a ditch, hit by a car, taken by—'

'Stop right there,' she cut in. 'I know you're panicking. Of course you are. You're his dad. But you know Ryan. He's logical. He'll go somewhere that he likes. Somewhere where he's been happy.'

'That's why I thought he'd come to you. Because he loves you.' He refused to listen to his heart's plaintive whine. *And so do I.*

'I'll check with Security.' Claire tapped a number into the phone and spoke rapidly to the head of security. Her face was grim when she hung up. 'Nothing. They'll keep us posted if they spot him—I've given them my mobile number. OK. So he's not at home and he's not here. Where else would he go?'

'I don't know.' Panic seemed to have frozen his brain. 'I don't know.'

'Somewhere he feels safe. Somewhere he's been happy.' She chewed her lip thoughtfully. 'Have you tried Ally's?'

'No. I was just so sure he'd be here, that he'd come to find you.' *Because he misses you as much as I do.* Eliot pushed the thought away. No. There was no going back. Even though seeing her again made him want to hold her. And he wanted her to hold him back. Hold him tightly and reassure him that Ryan was safe, that he'd come home. That they were both back home with *her*.

'Right. Let's start with Ally. If he's not there, we'll make a list.'

How could she be so cool and calm about it? Why wasn't she doing the headless chicken thing, too?

Because Ryan wasn't her flesh and blood. He wasn't *her* child, his common sense pointed out.

'I'll ring Ally,' he said hoarsely, and Claire handed the phone to him.

But Ryan wasn't there either.

'Where else could he be?'

'My cottage?' Claire suggested.

Eliot nodded. 'I'll...' His voice snagged. 'I'll check,' he forced out.

Claire logged off her computer. 'Hold on. I'm coming with you.'

No, she wasn't. Much as he wanted her there, it wasn't a good idea. He was trying to get over her. Being with her again would throw him right back where he'd started. Wanting her. Missing her.

Where he'd started. Where he still was.

'It's not your problem.'

'Oh, yes, it is. Whether you like it or not, I love Ryan. I know he's not my son, but I still love him. And what happened between you and me doesn't change that.' She lifted her chin. 'Besides, I gave Security my mobile number, not yours. And two heads are going to be better than one at finding him.'

'You're on duty.'

'They'll have to manage without me. Ryan's more important than work.'

He stared at her for a moment. She meant it. She really meant it.

But when they reached his car, it had been clamped.

Eliot swore. 'I only parked here a few minutes ago!'

'Without a ticket,' she pointed out drily.

'I thought I'd get a fine.'

'They introduced clamping last week.'

Eliot swore again. 'I haven't got time to sort this out. I'll ring a taxi.' He pulled his mobile phone from his pocket.

'We'll take my car,' Claire said. 'You're not in a fit state to drive anyway.'

She was right. And he knew it. 'Thank you,' he said hoarsely.

But Ryan wasn't at Claire's cottage. He wasn't sitting on the doorstep, he wasn't in the back garden and there was no way he could have got into the house.

'Vi's?' Claire suggested. 'He might have gone to see Bess.' Ryan had adored the dog Claire had half-shares in and had spent ages trying to teach her tricks.

No luck there either. From the look on her face, Vi was clearly dying to ask if they'd sorted their problems out and were back together again, though to Eliot's relief she didn't say it.

'We need caffeine,' Claire said.

'We haven't got time to stop for coffee,' Eliot muttered through clenched teeth. 'We have to find my son.'

'Running around in a panic isn't going to help us find him. We need a list. Something we can work through, logically, tick off one by one. Have you called the police?'

'No,' Eliot admitted.

'Then you call them while I make us a coffee,' Claire said firmly.

By the time she handed him a mug, he'd given the police a description of Ryan. 'Chocolate biscuits?' he asked, curling his lip when she offered him the packet.

'You might not need chocolate, but I sure as hell do,' Claire said.

He saw that her hands were shaking—she was as scared as he was. She was just trying harder not to show it. He took the biscuits from her and held her hands tightly. 'We'll find him.'

'Of course we will,' she said.

She knew they were both lying. Both panicking. Both thinking about what might have happened to Ryan. Both blaming themselves, sure that they could have stopped Ryan running away if only they'd sat down and talked things through...

'There's no chance he would have gone to Malandra's?' Claire asked carefully.

Eliot shook his head. 'It's going to be tough enough to persuade him to even see her again.'

'Ouch. Maybe I could...' She stopped herself. No, she couldn't try meeting Malandra with Ryan and help them form the early bonds of their relationship. She couldn't get involved again. Couldn't torment herself that much. Because Eliot and Ryan were never going to be hers.

'Our list,' she said. 'Places we enjoyed. The science centre in Ludbury—we went to the planetarium there. The cinema. Pizza Presto.' The night Eliot had bought her roses.

'The toyshop—the one that's got the huge K'nex display in the window,' Eliot said.

'And the train station. He loves the trains.'

Eliot shuddered. 'No. He wouldn't have gone to London. He wouldn't.' The Natural History Museum, the Tower of London, the British Museum—Ryan had memorised the tube map, knew the stops and how to get to the buildings. But he wouldn't realise that they were closed. And London was no place for a seven-year-old to wander around alone.

Claire had already grabbed the phone and was frantically punching in the number of the railway station.

'Not there,' she said shakily. 'But I've given them my mobile number—they'll ring us if they spot him.'

'Your mobile…it *is* switched on?' Eliot asked.

She nodded. 'Since we left the hospital.'

'He couldn't have gone to Ludlow. You went by car so he wouldn't know the bus route.'

Claire moistened her dry lips. 'The register office. The hotel.'

Their wedding.

The start of their temporary marriage.

She met Eliot's gaze and it was as full of pain as her heart. Though she knew it was for a different reason. He regretted the beginning; she was the one who regretted the end.

'We'll start at the science centre,' Eliot said.

They worked through their list, place by place. He wasn't at any of them. Nobody they asked had seen a small boy wandering around on his own.

'Supposing he wasn't on his own,' Eliot said.

'No.' Claire took his hand and squeezed it, guessing what he was worrying about. The unspoken terror every parent had every time their child went out alone. 'He doesn't even talk to people unless he knows them. He wouldn't have gone off with someone.'

'He doesn't have any fear,' Eliot corrected. 'He wouldn't know that someone might—

might…' He choked the words off, clearly not wanting to voice his suspicions in case they came true. Horribly, horribly true.

'Even so, he wouldn't even talk to a stranger, let alone anything else. He's somewhere. We just have to find him. Maybe…maybe he went to the hospital, saw I wasn't there and went home again.'

Somehow she was still holding his hand when they walked back to the car. And he reached for her the minute she parked outside his house and got out of the car. Held her close while they checked the porch, the garden. Checked with the neighbours. Rang Ally again.

'He can't have vanished,' Eliot said, his eyes haunted. He held onto Claire as if he were drowning and only she could keep him afloat. 'He can't have just vanished.'

'Let's try my place again,' Claire said. 'And if he's not there, we'll talk to the radio stations, the newspapers, anyone who can spread the word and help us find him.'

Ryan wasn't sitting in Claire's porch. Or in Claire's garden. And it had started to rain, a thin drizzle that soaked swiftly through their clothes.

'Wherever he is,' Eliot said, 'he's cold and wet and lonely. Frightened. We have to find him, Claire. We have to.'

She held his hand tightly. 'We will. Look, it's too dark to see properly. Let's get a torch. There's one in the glove compartment of my car.'

Almost as soon as she'd said it, Eliot was back with the torch. He shone it round the garden. Nothing.

And then Claire heard a bang.

'What was that?' she asked.

Eliot shone the torch around the garden again. The light breeze had caught the door of her shed, blowing it slightly open and banging it shut. 'Just the shed.'

Hope flared so brightly—please, please don't let it be a false hope, she begged. Let it be Ryan. She took a deep breath. 'I never leave the shed door open.'

CHAPTER FOURTEEN

'PLEASE. Please let it be him,' Eliot whispered. 'My son. My little boy. Please let it be him.'

And then they opened the shed door fully. Eliot shone the torch into the tiny wooden structure. And they saw Ryan curled up asleep on one of the padded recliner chairs Claire used in the garden.

Eliot dropped the torch and pulled Claire into his arms. 'Thank you,' he said softly. 'Thank you.' And then he was kissing her and she was kissing him back, until they were both gasping for air.

'Who's there?' a small, sleepy voice quavered.

Claire broke the kiss. 'Ryan, it's Claire. Claire and Daddy. We've been so worried about you!'

Eliot scooped his son into his arms. 'We looked everywhere for you.'

'Are you angry?' Ryan asked.

'No. Well, yes,' Eliot admitted. 'You should never go out on your own like that. Anything could have happened to you. You could have got hurt.'

'But I wanted to see Claire,' Ryan protested. 'And when I asked you, you said she was at work. Away. I knew she wasn't away. Jed and Ally came here yesterday for tea. Jed told me. So I thought I'd come here for tea on my own and see Claire.'

'Except I really was at work,' she said gently.

'And it was cold. So I sat in the shed to wait for you to come home. Except you didn't. And then I fell asleep.'

She squeezed his hand. 'You're cold. Do you want me to get you some warm milk?'

'I should—' Eliot began, but was silenced by her glare as she switched on her kitchen light.

She heated some milk and poured it just the way Ryan liked it, then handed him the cup. 'So how did you get here?'

'On the bus.'

Ryan recited the exact route and Claire couldn't suppress her smile. 'Well, I know who to ask next time I'm lost! But seriously, Ryan, you shouldn't just go somewhere with-

out telling someone where you're going. Your
dad's been worried sick. So have I.'

'But I wanted to see you,' Ryan said. 'I
missed you. Why did you go away?'

'I had to, sweetheart. But I missed you, too.'

'Is it because of her? The one who says
she's my mummy?'

'The one who *is* your mummy,' Claire corrected. 'Malandra's your mother.'

'But she's not married to Daddy. *You* are.
And I don't want her. I want you,' Ryan said.

'It's very complicated,' she hedged, throwing Eliot a 'help me' look.

'And you're tired. I'll get you home to bed,'
Eliot said.

Ryan's lower lip thrust out. 'No.' He folded
his arms. 'I want to stay here.'

'Tell you what,' Claire said, 'how about you
go and have a nap upstairs for now—and then
we'll talk about it later?'

'Grown-ups always say that,' Ryan grum-
bled.

'I'll take you upstairs,' Eliot said.

Ryan shook his head. 'No. I want Claire.'

Eliot shrugged, but his eyes showed how
hurt he was by his son's rejection. Claire
mouthed at him, 'Don't take it personally—he

doesn't mean that. He's just upset and tired.' She took Ryan upstairs and put him to bed. She sat with him, holding his hand until he fell asleep, then went downstairs to face Eliot.

'I didn't plan any of this,' she said, seeing the black look on his face. 'So I'd advise you not to start throwing any accusations.'

'I'm not going to. I just wanted to know he was safe, that was all.'

Even though he knew his son was perfectly safe now, the worry was still etched into the lines round his eyes. Worry and misery and longing and...

No. She was seeing what she wanted to be there, what she dreamed was there. It wasn't love. Not for her. That kiss in the garden hadn't meant anything. It had just been relief, a release of pent-up tension and fear from their search. Eliot didn't want her. He'd rejected her, hadn't he? Rejected her as soon as she'd told him she couldn't have a baby. That she'd had chlamydia. That she wasn't pristine and perfect.

'Ryan talks about you a lot. He misses you,' Eliot said.

Claire felt tears gather at the back of her eyes and couldn't trust herself to speak. She missed the little boy, too. And his father. She'd missed Eliot so much. Missed the way he held her, missed the feel of his skin, missed his scent. Missed the teasing and the laughter and the love…

But she was deluding herself. Eliot didn't love her. Not really.

He sighed. 'I miss you, too.'

'You'll get used to it.' She forced her voice to sound hard, uncaring.

'It doesn't feel like it.'

'It's over, Eliot.'

'It doesn't have to be.'

'That's what Paddy said.'

'Paddy?'

'My ex-husband. But I couldn't live with him any more. It took me a long, long time to forgive him for taking away my choices.'

'He took away your—?' Eliot broke off, flushing.

Shock rippled through her when she realised what he must have been thinking. 'You thought *I* gave it to Paddy? You thought *I'd* been the one sleeping around?' She shook her head in disbelief. How could he possibly have thought that about her?

The fact he could think it proved that he didn't love her. Because you never, ever thought the worst about someone you loved. 'I think you'd better leave. I'll bring Ryan back to you in the morning.'

'Claire—no, wait. I don't know what I thought. I was mixed up.'

'You can say that again.' Her voice was laced with bitterness.

'Why didn't you tell me right from the start? The truth, I mean? Why didn't you trust me?'

'Because I felt dirty. Embarrassed. *Ashamed.* I didn't even tell my best friend.' She rubbed her hand across her face, as if to make herself feel clean. 'So what was I supposed to say to you? How was I supposed to tell you that I was such a hopeless wife that my husband looked elsewhere—and then he'd given me a sexually transmitted disease that had made me unable to have children?'

'But it wasn't your fault. You trusted Paddy and you didn't have any symptoms. How were you supposed to know?'

'I'm a doctor. I'm supposed to know everything,' she said tightly. 'Including the fact that my husband was completely incapable of remaining faithful. And even though he promised it wouldn't happen again, it did. I don't know how many times and I don't want to know. I only found out about the last one when I'd taken his mobile phone instead of mine by mistake, and she texted him. It was a very *personal* message. OK, so I shouldn't have read it. But I did. And that was the end for me. I left him.'

Eliot reached out for her. 'Oh, Claire.'

She gritted her teeth. 'Don't touch me.' She couldn't bear his pity now. Not after what they'd shared. Not after what they'd lost.

'I apologise. Unreservedly and from the bottom of my heart. I'm sorry, Claire. We've had a lot of crossed wires between us, made some stupid mistakes—most of all not trusting each other. But listen to me. Please.' He cupped her face in his hands. 'I love you.'

She backed away, knowing that his touch could undo her. She had to be strong. For both their sakes. 'That's what you told the judge. Because you thought it was what he wanted to hear.'

'No. You told me to tell the truth,' he reminded her. 'So I did. I told the world I loved you.'

'But you never said it to me. The first I knew of it was when you said it in the middle of a law court. In front of strangers.' She shook her head. 'That hurts, Eliot. It hurts because you didn't trust me enough to say it to me first.'

'I was scared I'd frighten you away. I didn't think you felt the same way that I did. I didn't want to lose you— Oh, hell, I don't know what I was thinking. I've screwed up, big time. I know that. But I love you, Claire. And I thought if I loved you enough, you might grow to love me back.'

Oh, she did. *She did.*

'And after we made love… I thought you knew how I felt about you. Night after night, I told you with my body. Showed you how much I loved you.'

Just as, night after night, she'd told him the same thing in exactly the same way.

But there was too much stacked up against them. It could never work. She lifted her chin. 'We agreed on a temporary marriage.'

Eliot's eyes were very clear. 'I don't want a temporary marriage.'

'That's why I'm giving you a divorce. So you can find someone who can give you a brother or sister for Ryan, make a real family for him.'

He shook his head. 'I don't want someone else. I want you.'

'But I can't give you a child. Not naturally, anyway. And even if we tried IVF, there are no guarantees. The odds aren't that good. We could go through months and months of treatment and longing and misery and it still might not work. I don't think I can handle that.'

'You don't have to. But don't walk away from me, Claire. I love you. I want you. It doesn't matter that we can't have a baby together. We have Ryan—and he loves us both. That's enough. We're a family.'

Easy enough to say. But did he mean it?

He kissed the pulse at the inside of her wrist. 'I don't want to be without you any more, Claire. My life's been so empty since you left.'

'You let me walk away.'

'Because I thought you didn't love me. Because I thought I'd made exactly the same mistake as I'd made with Malandra—fallen in love with someone who didn't love me enough to stay with me, be my love for the rest of our lives. When you told me you couldn't have children, I thought...' He sighed. 'Well, I thought you'd only wanted Ryan. That you'd only wanted me for what I could give you—a ready-made family.'

She could see the pain in his eyes. The hurt at being rejected. The same hurt she'd felt when he'd walked out on her. He'd thought she didn't want him. 'It wasn't like that.'

'It felt like it. And it hurt like hell.'

'You were the one who resigned,' she pointed out. 'You were the one who walked away from the hospital without even saying goodbye to me.'

'What else could I do? It was tearing me apart, seeing you at work and knowing you weren't mine any more. Remembering what we'd shared, missing you, wanting you back in my arms. Back in my heart. Back in my life.' He swallowed. 'Hell. If I wasn't already married to you, I'd propose. Offer you everything I have to give. Heart and soul, for the rest of our lives. But since you *are* married to me... I don't know what to say.'

'Neither do I.' She stared at him, hardly able to believe what he'd just said. That he'd asked her to marry him all over again. That he wanted her, heart and soul, for the rest of their lives. He really, really wanted her.

'Come back to me, Claire. Let's start again. And this time do it properly.'

Tempting. So, so tempting. But she couldn't give in to that temptation. It wasn't fair on him. 'I can't. I can't give you what you want,' she whispered.

'Yes, you can. Because I want you, Claire Slater. I want *you*.'

'Even though I can't give you a family?'

'We *are* a family. You, me and Ryan.'

'Eliot…'

'I'm not like Paddy. I keep my promises. You can trust me. Just as I know I can trust you. And, yes, I realise neither of us is very good at this trusting someone business—we've both done it in the past, got it wrong and been hurt. But we can learn to trust again if we do it together.'

'You think so?'

'I *know* so.' He smiled at her. 'But first I have a question.'

'Which is?'

'Do you love me, Claire?'

'I told you I did.'

'When?'

'Every night. When you were asleep,' she admitted. 'And every time I told you…' The image zoomed straight back to her. How she'd whispered her love in the night. 'You smiled.'

'Tell me now I'm awake.'

'I love you.'

He smiled. 'And I love you, Claire Slater. For the rest of our lives.'

EPILOGUE

Six months later.

'OK. YOU can take the blindfold off now,' Claire directed.

Ryan looked at his new bedroom. The blue walls, the star-shaped lampshade, the hand-made curtains with the constellations stitched onto them in exactly the right places. And then he looked up at the ceiling. 'Wow. You even painted the solar system on my ceiling! Oh, Mum!' He hugged her.

'Happy birthday, son.' She hugged him back.

'Can I show my other mummy? At the weekend?' he asked.

'Sure. She'll be ringing you in the next half-hour to wish you a happy eighth birthday and tell you what she's got planned for you for the weekend,' Eliot said, sliding his arms round his wife's waist. 'And then we're taking you to the pictures.'

'And after that we're going out for a pizza,' Claire added.

'And this time, Mrs Slater, I'm not just going to kiss you goodnight in the car,' Eliot murmured in her ear.

She tipped her head back to grin at him. 'That'd better be a promise.'

'It is,' he assured her, his eyes dancing with a mixture of teasing and desire.

And love. This was what it felt like, Claire thought. To be part of a family. A family of her own. The three of them, a family at last.

MEDICAL ROMANCE™

Large Print

Titles for the next six months…

May

THE POLICE DOCTOR'S SECRET   Marion Lennox
THE RECOVERY ASSIGNMENT   Alison Roberts
ONE NIGHT IN EMERGENCY   Carol Marinelli
CARING FOR HIS BABIES   Lilian Darcy

June

ASSIGNMENT: CHRISTMAS   Caroline Anderson
THE POLICE DOCTOR'S DISCOVERY   Laura MacDonald
THE MIDWIFE'S NEW YEAR WISH   Jennifer Taylor
A DOCTOR TO COME HOME TO   Gill Sanderson

July

THE FIREFIGHTER'S BABY   Alison Roberts
UNDERCOVER DOCTOR   Lucy Clark
AIRBORNE EMERGENCY   Olivia Gates
OUTBACK DOCTOR IN DANGER   Emily Forbes

MILLS & BOON®

Live the emotion

0405 LP 2P P1 Medical

MEDICAL ROMANCE™

 *Large Print*

August

EMERGENCY AT INGLEWOOD	Alison Roberts
A VERY SPECIAL MIDWIFE	Gill Sanderson
THE GP'S VALENTINE PROPOSAL	Jessica Matthews
THE DOCTORS' BABY BOND	Abigail Gordon

September

HIS LONGED-FOR BABY	Josie Metcalfe
EMERGENCY:	
A MARRIAGE WORTH KEEPING	Carol Marinelli
THE GREEK DOCTOR'S RESCUE	Meredith Webber
THE CONSULTANT'S SECRET SON	Joanna Neil

October

THE DOCTOR'S RESCUE MISSION	Marion Lennox
THE LATIN SURGEON	Laura MacDonald
DR CUSACK'S SECRET SON	Lucy Clark
HER SURGEON BOSS	Abigail Gordon

MILLS & BOON®

Live the emotion

0405 LP 2P P2 Medical